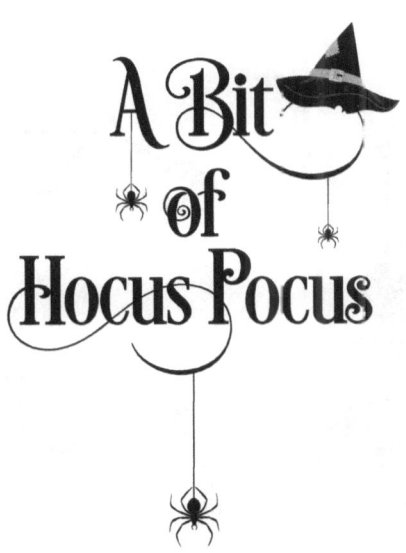

A Bit of Hocus Pocus

HOLIDAZE IN SALEM

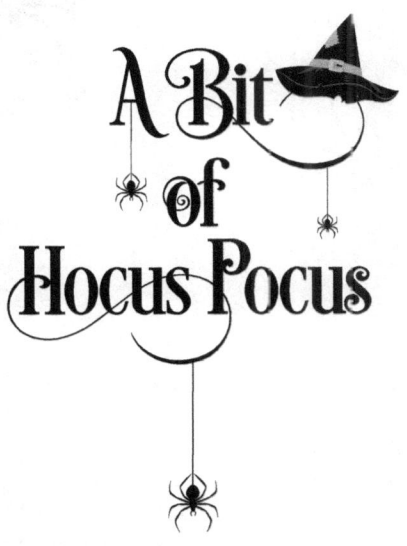

A Bit of Hocus Pocus

HOLIDAZE IN SALEM

KELLY ELLIOTT

A Bit of Hocus Pocus
Book 1 Holidaze in Salem © 2022 by Kelly Elliott

Cover Design by: Graphics by Stacy
Interior Design & Formatting by: Elaine York,
Allusion Publishing, www.allusionpublishing.com
Copy and Proofing Edits by: Andrea Vanryken with Yellow Bird
Editing

For more information on Kelly and her books, please visit her
website www.kellyelliottauthor.com.

A Bit of Witchy History

Before we begin, I need you to know a little something first. *There are witches in my family.*

Ever since I was a little girl, my Aunt Lucy has told the same story to me and my sister, Sarah, of how we are from a long-descended line of witches. The most famous one being our eleventh great-grandmother, Sarah Wildes, who was hung in Salem, Massachusetts, during the Salem witch trials. And the best part of the story was how Sarah was named after that famous witch. Okay, that was the best part for my sister, not for me. And that wasn't even true. Every first-born female on my mother's side of the family has been named Sarah, but, hey, I never argued with my aunt or sister on that little detail. Don't worry—my mother gave my father dibs on naming the second born. Me! Thank goodness my father named me after his grandmother, Hollie. Who I might add, was not a witch. At least, I don't think she was.

Back to the story.

My favorite part of my aunt's story had always been that our mother married a man with the last name of Craft.

According to my Aunt Lucy, it had been fate that the two of them met and fell in love. What a perfect last name for my mother. Elaine Craft. Get it? With my mother coming from a long line of witches... Hello, destiny! I'd like to introduce you to fate. I should mention, my aunt has yet to find any history of witches on my father's side of the family. But with a name like Craft, there had to be at least one, right? At least, that was her way of thinking as well as that of my sisters. My father, Mike Craft, likes to tease that there are indeed witches in the family because everyone has a little bit of magick in them.

According to Aunt Lucy, it was meant to be that my parents met and fell in love in high school. That their love stayed strong while both went off to college, even though Aunt Lucy swears it was because my mother put a love spell on my father—which my mother has not denied, I might add, nor has she confirmed this part of the story. My father says one day, while walking down the hall on his way to first period, he spotted my mother and felt like someone sucker-punched him. He was in love from that moment on. It was a sweet gesture, and one that I had wanted to happen to me, that I believed would happen to me. Well, until I grew up and realized that events like that were few and far between.

Anyhoo, they fell in love, and today, they are the parents of three kids. The oldest, Sarah, who is thirty-three. Next, me, Hollie, twenty-nine, and last, my brother, Nathan, who just turned twenty-five. All of whom my aunt Lucy has declared as witches. Sarah is totally on board. Nathan, he's on the fence about it all. I really think it depends on his mood. And me... well...let's just say I stopped believing in all that hocus pocus when I realized the world wasn't such a nice place.

But back to the witches in the family.

Let me give you a bit of history on the family. Hang with me for just a bit; I know you're excited to hear about my little journey.

My mother's family immigrated from Chipping Norton, a small market town west of Oxfordshire, England. Where, according to both my mother and aunt, the women of the family were rumored to hold special powers. They were healers, and if someone was sick or suffering from an ailment, they went to their herb garden and worked their...*magick*. Once they came to the US, they continued to be one with the earth, but this time, they wouldn't be called healers like they had been back in England.

My father's family was from a small seaside town called Laugharne in Dyfed. They come from a long line of fishermen. Nothing really exciting to report on Dad's side of the family. My father is still a fisherman to this day and a damn good one. He takes people out on fishing charters and has won numerous fishing championships. We're all proud of him, especially my mother. She adores my father, just as he does her.

Both towns are on my list of places to visit one day. My mother and Aunt Lucy have gone back to England to meet with relatives. Rumor has it, we're related to the queen. Sixth cousins, seventh-removed, or something like that? What does that even mean? Removed from what? All I know is, it hasn't done me a bit of good. It's not like I can say, "Hey...let me plan the next royal wedding because we're sixth cousins removed over half a dozen times!" Oh, I haven't mentioned I'm a party planner. A darn good one at that, if I do say so myself.

I'm sorry.... I digressed a bit.

My sister, Sarah, loved the stories of our witch lineage growing up, and I did as well, until I...well, until I grew up, like I said. Then they simply became silly stories that I no longer had time to entertain. Okay, I will admit it might have something to do with the silly curse I tried to put on Lucas Dayton in first grade after he called me a crybaby. It didn't work at all, and my heart had been broken. If I was a witch, I sucked at it.

Aunt Lucy would say I was so much like my mother, whereas Sarah was more like Aunt Lucy. Sarah would go and spend time at my aunt's store nearly every day, perfecting her "craft." I, on the other hand, spent countless hours with my nose in books. Not the kind of books Sarah and Aunt Lucy studied. I was passionate about reading, just not books about magickal spells. I will admit that every now and then, you'd find me reading a book about witches, but the fictional kind. On my nightstand growing up was *Harry Potter*. On Sarah's, *The History of Paganism* or *A Guide to Magical Herbs and Spells*. Once or twice, I even caught her and my mother in Mom's greenhouse with their heads bent over some herb and my mother telling her all the wonderful things that it was used for. I never really got Mom's obsession with herbs; she hated to cook.

Back to the differences between me and Sarah. I lit candles from Bath & Body Works. Sarah lights white sage and lavender smudge sticks. Whatever floats your boat, I say. I love my sister and aunt dearly, but witches? Nah.

Let's fast-forward to present day, shall we? I run a successful party planning business in our hometown of Salem. Yes, our family still lives in Salem, and yes, we were forced to go to the Salem Witch Museum every year for a school trip. I mean, if you asked me, I would have rather gone to Boston and seen the art museums, or cool things like that. Oh, and lunch at Legal Sea Foods. Have you had their Bang Bang Cauliflower? It's amazing. I'm going off-track again. Like I said, I own a party planning company called Holidaze in Salem. Cute, huh? Sarah works at Aunt Lucy's store. The Covens Magick Cottage. And no, magick is not spelled wrong. If you were a witch, you'd know that that is the way witches spell magick—with a "k" to differentiate it from stage magic. You're welcome for that bit of information!

You may be wondering why I'm telling you all of this. You're going to need this info in a bit, once you read all about me standing in a living room with my best friend, Kristin Mills, a spell book in her hands and me holding a Halloween bat. It will make sense, I promise. I should mention, we're both drunk. I know...I know.... But I'm not a witch, you say! Well, I was pushed to the brink by, of all things...a man. Yes, a man. I'm about to let my best friend talk me into putting a spell on him. Lucas Dayton. I know, I went down this road before in first grade, remember? It didn't work out so well then either.

Lucas has been a thorn in my side for as long as I can remember. First grade, to be exact. A man whom I love to hate and am secretly in love with. The problem is...Lucas doesn't like me very much. So, in my drunken state, I was talked into putting what I thought was a spell on him to make him like me just enough to stop making my life miserable, with the constant bickering we do back and forth. Instead, the spell we put on him was... You know what? I'll just let you read the story. You'll soon find out how this little adventure veers off in a direction I never thought it would. We're not starting in my living room with me drunk; let's take it back to earlier in the day.

It's just a bit of hocus pocus, you guys....

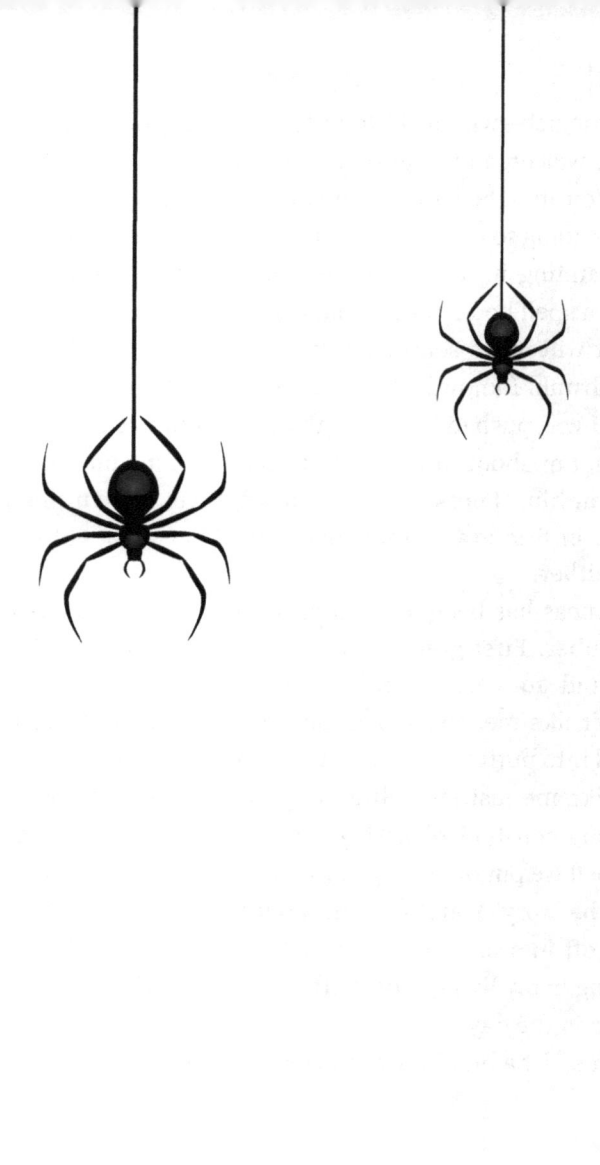

Chapter One

Hollie

I stepped back and smiled as I looked at my handiwork. "Pretty darn cute, if I do say so myself," I whispered as I let my eyes take in the room.

"Hollie! Oh, my goodness!" a voice said from behind me. "It looks beautiful, sweetheart!"

Turning, I grinned as I saw the host of the party walk up. Rose Dayton. I'd known her since I was a little girl and had always adored her. The fact that she hired me to set up her fall-themed book club party was an honor. I had dived into this project head-first, full of excitement. Fall was, after all, my favorite time of year. Especially in Salem. And this was Rose, one of my favorite clients. I'd done a number of parties and events for her, so I felt honored that she kept asking me back to plan more. I'd even, though I'd never wanted to admit it to myself, always secretly hoped to see her son, Lucas.

Looking back at my handy work, I sighed. I had poured my heart into this one simply because it had been for Rose. My eyes swept over the room again. On the table was a beautiful yet simple fall centerpiece that featured red apples I had used as little vases with fall flowers in them. Sage and copper greenery were on the table, along with a few books that had candles in small hurricane lamps placed on top of them.

"I'm glad you like it, Rose. It means a lot to me that you're happy with it all."

"Like it? I love it, Hollie. How in the world did you do that to the apples? Are those real flowers in there?"

Smiling with pride, I nodded. "They are! Just a simple little trick I use."

She reached down and picked up the small pinecone that had a slip of paper with a guest's name handwritten on it in calligraphy. She placed it back down on the sage-colored plates she had bought just for this party. "The placeholder cards are adorable. Everything is so perfect. No wonder you're the best in Salem. You never fail to outdo yourself."

I felt my cheeks blush. After working my ass off for the last six years, I had finally made it; I'd become one of the top event planners in Salem. I could do any kind of event asked of me. From newborn showers to retirement parties to everything in between. The City of Salem had even asked me to plan their big Christmas party for their employees this year. I was over the moon excited about that. If I did a good job on it, I was hoping they'd let me do next year's Salem Witches' Halloween Ball. My aunt and sister were on board, of course, but I'd never wanted to use my influence to get the job. I wanted my talent to win it for me.

I was best known for my romantic events like surprise engagements or anniversaries. I had to admit, those were my favorites. I was a sucker for a good romance story. Maybe because I was still looking for my own happily ever after.

Rose turned in a circle. Faux trees lined the walkway from the porch to the back patio and were covered in white lights, with Edison lights strung across the large trees in the backyard for when the sun set and the host needed to provide light in the backyard.

In the yard were large beanbag chairs, each with a blanket placed over it, along with the book that Rose's book club had been reading. In the middle was a fire pit ready to go with a push of a button. Small s'mores kits were also placed on a small table that sat in front of each beanbag, along with a cup that had a small bag of hot chocolate and mini-marshmallows in it. All they would need to do is add hot water.

"In each s'mores kit is a small skewer that opens up for them to roast the marshmallows on. They also have their names on them, and each blanket has the name on it as well so they should be able to find their chairs with no problem," I said as I walked toward the other seating area in the yard. "You mentioned the gift idea would be left up to me, so I hope you like that."

"You thought of everything!" Rose gushed. "I love the gifts! How do you come up with such cute ideas?"

Simply smiling, I wanted to say, when I had an open checkbook to work with, I could make anything amazing. And for this job, the hostess was attempting to make her fall book club meeting outshine any other member's, past or future. I loved Rose to pieces, though. So, when she told me to outshine last year's book club fall party, I had tried my best. Rose's husband, Tim, was a doctor in town and sat on the city council. He had given me my first big solo event to plan, and I would forever be grateful to him for it.

"Your guests should be arriving soon, so I'll get on out of here. Is there anything else you need from me?"

She beamed back at me. "No, everything looks amazing, Hollie. Thank you so much."

I kissed her cheek and said, "It's my pleasure."

As I headed through the courtyard, I slid open the back door and stepped inside Rose's house. Quickly making my way through the large, historical home, I grabbed my laptop bag and purse and started for the front door. Though everyone knew Rose would not have thrown this altogether herself, I would never stay at the event unless asked to.

Opening the door, I stepped outside and quickly made my way down the steps and sidewalk and to my car that was parked in front of the house.

Just as I went to open the car door, I heard my name and instantly knew who it was. His voice irritated and thrilled me at the same time. More so the latter.

Slowly turning on my heels, I was met by those caramel-colored eyes that made my insides want to melt. I made the mistake of letting my gaze drop to his mouth and nearly moaned when he smiled that crooked smile. And that stupid, stupid, dimple of his. Ugh. It didn't often come out, but when it did, my lady bits went crazy.

Lucas Dayton.

I drew in a breath and tried my best to not let any emotions show. I was rather good at it since I'd had years of pretending to not like the man whom I had way more naughty dreams about than I cared to admit.

"Hey, Lucas. What brings you by Rose's house?"

The moment the question was out of my mouth, I wanted to crawl into a hole. Did he really need a reason to be at his own mother's house?

He laughed. "Well, she is my mother, so there is that."

I wanted to punch myself but somehow managed to play it off. "I wasn't aware you were part of her romance book club."

He froze and I internally fist-pumped. "Shit," he hissed. "Is that today?"

"Yep. Better get on in there before you miss any of the book talk."

I turned, opened the door, and was about to slip inside the safety of my car when he grabbed hold of my door and kept me from closing it.

"What brings you here?" he asked.

"If you must know, I helped your mom plan the event and was making sure all the decorations and such were in order."

He let his gaze move over my face before his eyes met mine. I hated the way I felt, like I wanted to squirm in my own skin when he stared at me like that. I could never read the man, and that drove me crazy because I could read everyone. And when I say that, I mean it. Lucas was the only person whose thoughts eluded me. I could never tell what he was thinking. At times, I swore I could read minds, I was so good at guessing a person's thoughts. Not with him, though.

"Is there something you needed?" I asked as I tried to keep my voice calm and steady.

He smirked. "Why aren't you in the book club, Hollie? You don't like romance books?"

I forced a smile. "I'm not over fifty, Lucas. Therefore, this really isn't my kind of crowd."

One brow rose and I knew he was about to say something awful like I acted like a fifty-year-old woman or dressed like one. Something rude would no doubt slip free from those soft and plump-looking lips. I wondered how soft they would feel to anyone he kissed. I jerked my eyes up to his nose.

Do not look at his mouth, Hollie, do not do it.

We continued to just stare at one another, neither of us wanting to be the first to break eye contact and admit some weird defeat.

I wasn't even sure why Lucas and I bickered back and forth, always tossing insults. I mean, I understood why we did it when we were in school. We were constantly competing against each other for one thing or another. He couldn't possibly still be bitter because I kicked his ass at nearly everything we went up against each other on. I smiled, thinking back to those days.

A race, boys against girls in first grade, and I had kicked his little five-year-old ass. Then in second grade, it was a contest to see who could throw and make the most baskets on the basketball court. I won that time too. Third grade, it had been another foot race, this time, just between the two of us. I came out victorious in that race as well. Fourth grade, he finally beat me at something and got first place in the science project. Fifth grade went back to me when I won the spelling bee contest. Sixth grade, I took home the best overall student of the year award. It continued like that all through middle and high school. No matter what was on the line, my goal in life was to beat Lucas, and his was the same. I had to win because if I didn't, he would never let me live it down. And I had worked my ass off to beat him at almost everything. Then came senior year when Lucas and I were both up for valedictorian. It was literally a race to the finish, with Lucas beating me out by .5 points. The bickering grew worse after that, and I thought for sure it would stop when we graduated, became adults. I was wrong. A part of me enjoyed it, though, and I had a feeling he did as well. Except while I kept up my end of the bickering simply to be able to talk to him, he did it because he...well...he didn't like me. That bothered me more than anything if I'm being honest. It really sucks being in love with a man who doesn't feel the same way. Hell, who doesn't even like you. Everyone liked me. Well, almost everyone. There was a small group of people from high school who did not like me or my sister, Sarah. Nathan was different. He was handsome, so all the girls liked him, and was the star quarterback of the football team. Sarah and I... We were labeled weird because of the whole witch history thing and because of Sarah practicing witchcraft with my aunt.

I shook those thoughts away.

"Before you toss out one of your insults, save it. I really don't have time, Lucas."

He feigned hurt. "Why, Hollie Craft, how do you know I wasn't going to say something nice?"

I let out a bark of laughter. "You? Say something nice to me? Hell has not frozen over yet. You've hated me for this long, I hardly think you would suddenly grow a fondness for me."

His smile faded and he reached for my hand. My heart felt like it stopped in my chest as a rush of pleasure reached through my body. "Hollie, I don't hate you. I—"

Before he could finish, Rose came rushing out of the house. "Hollie! Wait! I can't believe I forgot to ask you something!"

Lucas dropped my hand and turned to see his mother coming down the steps and toward us.

"Lucas! Darling! Did you already speak to Hollie about the secret engagement?"

My heart dropped as I shot my gaze back to Lucas. "En-engagement?"

He nodded. "Yeah."

Before I could even let my brain catch up to my mouth, I blurted out, "Who are you asking to marry you? I didn't think you were even dating anyone."

The moment his eyes sparkled with delight, I knew I had just made a gross error.

"Is that a bit of *jealousy* I hear in that voice of yours, Hollie? And are you keeping tabs on who I'm dating?"

A rush of awkward laughter came out of my mouth, and I quickly pressed my lips together before I said, "Please. If anything, I feel sorry for her. I hope she knows what she's getting into with you. Poor girl has no idea what a real..."

I let my voice trail off when I noticed Rose standing there with her brows lifted as she waited for me to throw out an insult to her younger son. I quickly shut my mouth.

He laughed. "As much as I would love to see where this was going, Hollie, the engagement surprise is not for me."

I was going to ignore the way that made my body feel relieved. "Who is it for then?"

"Greg!" Rose announced with a beam of happiness, clearly forgetting I had just been rude to her other son.

Lucas nodded. "Yep, it's for Greg."

"Greg's getting married?" I asked in shock. The last I heard he was happily playing the field.

"If she says yes," Lucas stated as Rose hit him in the stomach.

"Of course, she will say yes, but we need your help in making it the most romantic engagement in the history of engagements!"

Lucas rolled his eyes.

"Wow, that's a big request to fill," I said with a nervous giggle. "Um, how long have they been dating?"

Lucas answered, "Six months or so. Greg has put me in charge of taking care of things."

Nodding, I pulled my head back and stared at Lucas. "Why would he put you in charge of this? Seems to me like it would be your brother wanting to set this up."

Rose chuckled. "I thought the same thing, but he is so busy at the hospital and working so much overtime..."

"He called in a favor. I like Janet, and I think they both deserve something nice, so I agreed to do it."

I was momentarily stunned by how sweet it was that Lucas wanted to do that for his brother.

"And you thought of me to make that happen?" I asked in a skeptical voice. "You never think of me in a positive way, Lucas."

"What?" Rose asked as she turned an evil eye on her son.

His brows pulled in tight. "That's not true."

If I hadn't known better, I would have thought I hurt his feelings, but I knew better than that.

Rose started to speak. "Lucas suggested Wendy, but I told him that you were the better choice."

Why did that hurt so damn much? "I see." Lucas looked down at the ground and kicked at a small rock, not meeting my eyes. I should have known he would want her since they had dated off and on over the years. She wasn't a fan of mine either. All through my freshman year of high school, she had been nothing but a bully to me—until one day I grew tired of it and started standing up for myself.

Clearing my throat, I said, "Well, Wendy does have a lot of experience."

Rose laughed. "Not like you."

"She is Janet's sister, though," Lucas interjected. Then he sighed. "But when I mentioned her to Mom, she suggested you and said that you were the best."

"Well, that looked like it was hard to even say," I said with a smirk.

"It was," he agreed. Another hit in the stomach by Rose.

"You only thought of her because you've dated her," Rose stated.

My stomach clenched with a sick feeling. I was pretty sure their relationship was a "friends with benefits" kind of a thing, but I wasn't sure. It also didn't help that Wendy was also a party planner, not on the scale that I was, owning my own company and all, but she did her fair share of events. Mostly weddings, if I recalled correctly, and catering to out-of-towners who wanted that Salem experience. I never really paid attention to what she did because I never considered her competition. She seemed to like to do the more traditional Salem Witch-type events, which was fine by me. And I didn't like her. Petty, I know.

Lucas smirked as if he were reading my mind. Suddenly, the thought of working on this with him was too much to even think about.

I drew in a slow breath and exhaled before focusing back on Rose. "I'm sorry, Rose, I won't be able to help out."

She frowned. "Drat. Do you have something else planned for that day?"

It was only then that I realized I had no idea when this was supposed to be. I was about to say yes when I noticed Lucas lean forward, suddenly very interested in my reply. When I looked at him, I wanted to slap the smug look right off his face. He knew I had no idea when it was and had just lied.

"Yes, Hollie, do you have something planned for then?"

"When is it again?" I asked Rose as I glared at Lucas.

"They both love Halloween so much, so he'd like to ask her on Halloween. I'd like it to be Halloween-themed. Greg is going to tell her they are going to a custom party."

I loved Halloween-themed parties, especially when costumes were involved.

"Will it be a party also?" I asked.

"Yes, Greg wants it to be just them alone when he asks, with us close by, of course. Then everyone will join in on the celebration," Lucas said.

"I'm so sorry, Rose, but I already have two events that I'm organizing for Halloween day. I honestly don't think I could take on this project as well."

"Hollie, you're the only one I trust to make this special for Greg and Janet. I'll pay you double."

I shook my head. "It's not about the money, Rose. It's honestly about me not having enough time." It was the truth.

I had two Halloween-themed parties I was helping plan: one kids' event and the other, a very adult-themed party. I did have a small handful of employees, and I knew if I had it all planned out, I could do the surprise engagement and celebration after.

The heartbreak on her face nearly did me in. She forced a smile and gave me a slight nod. "I understand."

Lucas must have seen it as well because he took his mother's hands and brought them up to his mouth, kissing the back of both. It was the sweetest thing I'd ever seen him do.

"Don't worry, Mom. I promise you it will be special for them. If anyone deserves it, it's Greg."

I closed my eyes and struggled internally. Greg had fought for a number of years as a child with leukemia, and there was a moment in time when it wasn't certain whether he would make it. He fought like hell, and I remembered how torn up Lucas was over it. It was the only time we'd ever called a temporary ceasefire.

"I know you don't want to hire Wendy, but she plans all kinds of parties, and I'm sure she'll do a great job," Lucas stated.

Wendy would do a terrible job, and we all knew it. I was going to regret what I was about to say.

Forcing the words out of my mouth, I said, "I'll do it."

They both turned and looked at me—Rose with a smile and Lucas with a look of relief. Maybe he hadn't really wanted Wendy to do it after all.

"Are you sure? We don't want to stress you out, and if you're just doing it so Wendy doesn't get the job...," he started to say before I held up my hand. Anger pulsed through me.

"I could give a rat's ass about Wendy, Lucas. I'm doing this for your mother and Greg. That's it."

Rose threw herself into me and hugged me. "Thank you so much, Hollie! Thank you!"

Lucas sighed and ran his hand threw his hair. He had clearly not wanted Wendy to do the job—that much was obvious—but he also had tried to make it seem like he hadn't wanted me to do it either. The man was confusing as hell.

Rose stepped back and took my hand and her son's. "Now, you two figure out the best time to get together and plan this."

"What?" we both asked in unison.

"Greg asked you to do this, Lucas. Now, you're in great hands. I've got to go! I have a book club party to get back to!"

Lucas and I watched as Rose disappeared back into her house.

We looked at one another and realized at the same time that Rose had put our hands together. I instantly pulled my hand away.

"This should be fun," Lucas deadpanned.

"I have an idea—why don't you just let me make all the plans, and we can say you helped?"

He let out a bark of laughter. "Oh, hell, no. I want this to be perfect for Greg and Janet. And you already said you have other parties you're planning."

My arms folded across my chest. "Are you saying I can't do the job without your help?"

"That is exactly what I'm saying, Hollie. You turned this down until you heard Wendy was going to do it."

"I am doing it because I like your brother, and you and I both know Wendy will not be able to set something up like I can."

"I still want to be a part of this to make sure my brother has the best engagement possible."

"I'm sorry, dickhead, this is what I do for a living. I run a very successful business. I don't need you to babysit me."

"I want input on this, Hollie. It's my brother, and I want it to be perfect. So, you're going to have to just put your desire to be the best at everything away for a bit and learn to work with a partner on this one."

I gasped and took a step back. "I don't desire to be the best at everything. And is it a crime to want to do a good job, Lucas? To take pride in my work? I've worked my ass off over the years to build this business. It's called pride, and I'm sorry if that is a turnoff for you."

Something changed in his eyes. They turned dark, and for a moment I couldn't tear my gaze from them. It was only when he closed them and ran his hand down his face that my trance broke.

"When can we meet to talk about the engagement?" he asked. "Halloween is less than two weeks away."

I reached into my bag and pulled out my calendar.

"You have a paper calendar? Why not use your phone?"

I shot him a look that I hoped read that I wanted him to drop dead. "I have tomorrow afternoon open. We can meet for lunch at Turner's if you want. One sound okay?"

"One is fine. See you then."

He turned and headed up toward the front door of his mother's house.

"Enjoy book club!" I called out.

"Fuck," he mumbled and turned on his heels and started back down the street toward his car.

I couldn't help but laugh as I called out, "I should have just let you go in!"

Lucas held up his hand and shot me the middle finger.

My smile faded as I watched him for a few more moments before I slipped into my car.

Starting it, I drew in a long breath. Working closely with Lucas was going to be torture. Not because I thought he would interfere with my job—no, because I knew being so close to him would wreak havoc with my stupid emotions toward him.

"I'm so screwed."

As I drove away, I never saw Rose standing in the window looking out, a wide, triumphant grin on her face.

Chapter Two

Lucas

I stopped right outside of Turner's Seafood, drew in a long, deep breath, and exhaled.

"Dude, do I really have to go in there with you?" Shawn Roberts, my best friend of twenty-five years, asked.

"Yes. You do."

He rolled his eyes. "Listen, this weird thing you've had going on with Hollie ever since we were, what, six?"

"Five."

Staring at me with a blank expression, he closed his eyes, shook his head, then looked directly at me. "Whatever. It's stupid. You're thirty-fucking-years old now, Lucas. Just admit to Hollie you like her."

My mouth fell open, and I quickly looked around before stepping closer to him. "I do not like her."

He smirked. "You admitted to me that you did. That you wanted to—"

I pointed to him. "Don't even say it. I was drunk at the time, and I was twenty. That was ten years ago. It was... It was a thing, that's all."

He gave a one-shoulder shrug. "Dude, I'm not judging you. I'd have already gone after her if I didn't think you were secretly obsessed with her."

That little bit of information made my chest tighten. "What? You like Hollie?"

Shawn laughed. "Half of the guys we hang with like her, Lucas. No one will ask the poor girl out because they think you'll be pissed. Did you ever wonder why in high school, no guy ever asked her out? I mean, clearly, it wasn't because of her looks. She's smoking-hot and has a body."

I blinked a few times and tried to figure out what emotion I was feeling. Anger? Jealousy? Fear? *Wait—fear?* What in the hell?

"I don't... I don't care if one of you guys dates her," I bit out.

Shawn raised a single brow. "Really? If I was to go in there with you, have lunch, suffer through listening to a bunch of party-planning talk, then ask her out, you won't care."

I went to answer that I would care less if he asked her out, but nothing came out when I opened my mouth. Shawn gave me a knowing look, so I cleared my throat and lied.

"Shawn, I honestly do not care if you ask Hollie out."

He wore a skeptical look.

"Scout's honor."

"You were never a Boy Scout, Lucas."

It was my turn to roll my eyes. "Whatever. Come on, it's after one, and she'll think I stood her up."

Shawn followed me into the restaurant. It didn't take long to find Hollie. My breath caught in my throat like it did every single time I saw this woman. It had since I could remember.

Sitting at a table by herself, Hollie looked beautiful. Her light-brown hair was pulled up and piled on top of her head in one of those messy buns women wore all the time. A few loose strands hung down, and she was twirling one in her finger as she chewed on a pencil while staring down at the open notebook on the table.

When she looked up, her cobalt-blue eyes lit up, and I wanted to believe it was from simply seeing me, but I knew better. Hollie had this light about her, and everyone who knew her adored her—even with all the rumors around town about her family, especially her aunt and sister. It wasn't out of the ordinary for some to claim to be witches in Salem, but with their family history dating back to the witch trials, there was just something about them that seemed to make people think they were different. Not in a bad way. The family was adored by everyone who knew them. Just in a mysterious way.

Hollie smiled a polite smile, and I wasn't sure if it was for me or for Shawn. She had just a touch of makeup on because...well...honestly, she didn't need to wear any at all. She was that beautiful.

We walked up to the table, and Shawn reached down, giving her a quick hug and hello. I didn't want to admit to myself that it made my blood boil. They were friends, and it was something he'd done a thousand times before. Something was different now. Oh, he just admitted he liked her and wanted to ask her out. Yeah, that was what was different.

"Hi, Shawn. Was Lucas too afraid to come alone?" Hollie asked as she tilted her head and looked as if she wanted to stick her tongue out at me.

Shawn looked at me and laughed. "Well, Hollie, you are a bit scary, you know."

She winked at him, and I wanted to slap the fucking smile off my best friend's face.

"We were in a meeting together, and I invited him to have lunch with us. You don't mind, do you?" I asked as I sat down.

Hollie flashed Shawn another bright smile. "I don't mind at all."

Okay. Was she flirting with him? And why in the hell couldn't she smile at me like that?

Hollie handed me a menu. "I went ahead and ordered some scallops with bacon."

Staring at the appetizer sitting in front of us, I couldn't help but wonder if she had known that that was my favorite here. How would she know that, though?

"Oh, Lucas's favorite," Shawn said as he took one and popped the whole damn thing into his mouth.

Hollie gave me a questioning look. "Are they really?"

I nodded and placed one on the small plate in front of me. "They are indeed."

"Huh, I didn't know that. They're mine too."

All I could do was smile. I suddenly felt strange. Like I had no idea what to say or do around Hollie. Usually, I had a plethora of insults I could toss out. Not bad ones. I really did like her. Okay, I more than liked her. But I had never once been tongue-tied around her.

"Thanks for emailing me back with some of the details," she continued. "I think a spooky, glamorous theme is the perfect way to go. From what I know about Janet, she is really into Halloween. And we know Greg loves it."

Shawn laughed. "Greg lives for Halloween."

We both looked over at him. He held up his hands. "Sorry, I'll just sit over here and eat."

"You do that," I said as I shook my head and looked back at Hollie.

Hollie focused back on me. "So, let's talk first about the party after the fact. Do you want it to be a sit-down dinner, or do you want it more buffet-style?"

"I think buffet-style might keep it more casual, and I'm sure that's what Greg would want."

She nodded and wrote it down in her notebook. "I agree. Do we have an idea of how many people will be at the event?"

"Family and close friends only. I would say, maybe thirty?"

Another nod.

"Am I getting invited?" Shawn asked.

"No," I answered without even looking at him.

"What do you mean, no? I'm your best friend."

Turning to look at him, I smiled. "Exactly. You're my best friend, not Greg's. Now, his best friend will be there."

Hollie giggled, then covered her mouth with her hand and tried to look as if she was reading something in her notes.

"Anyway, back to the party," I said.

Hollie cleared her throat and nodded. "You said Greg wants it to be held in the family barn. If I remember, the walls in the barn are wide, wooden planks, right?"

Greg and Janet had met in that barn when Wendy had brought her over seven months ago to ride horses. They had hit it off, even though they had known each other from school. They spent the entire afternoon talking. So, it was only fitting that he would ask her to marry him there and then have the celebration afterward.

"Yes, they are."

She smiled and my chest felt tight. It was a genuine smile. One that wasn't laced with sarcasm or anything like that. I had to fight the urge to rub at the ache. It wasn't very often she gave me a genuine smile, and I found I wanted to make her give me another one.

"Okay, so, for the dessert table, I was thinking we can hang up a sign that says, 'falling in love,' and use some old wooden crates and such for décor."

I nodded.

"Then, down the middle of the barn, we can have two long tables—that should be enough for that many guests. It will be dressed more in an elegant fashion but still sticking with the Halloween theme. I'm thinking, rose gold candelabras with some greener and fall flowers. Black glasses for wine and for soft drinks or water. Rose gold plates with black silverware. Black napkins draped over the plates, and if you want to do name plates, we could do printed ones and wrap them around the silverware, or we could paint the names on little pumpkins that will sit on the table."

She looked up from what she was reading. "How does that sound so far?"

"Umm..."

"Freaking amazing. How will you get all this stuff?" Shawn asked.

She blushed and I hated that he had made that color appear on those beautiful cheeks of hers.

"I have a warehouse where I've bought things over the years. I pretty much have everything for fall and Halloween parties since I do them so often. I just need to make sure, if I'm doing more than one Halloween party, I don't commit the same items to two different parties. I have a pretty good system laid out. And I'm the only one who does the decorating, so there is no risk of things being double booked."

"That's amazing, Hollie. You've certainly worked hard at building your business," Shawn stated.

Smiling once again, she replied, "Thank you, Shawn."

I cleared my throat, and they both turned to look at me. "If you two are done...?"

Hollie's smile faded and a pained look crossed her face. I instantly felt like a jerk. "We'll have a drink area as well. Maybe even make a few little potions."

"Potions? What kind of potions?" I asked.

She laughed. "Regular drinks, like tea or sangria, and just name them something cute. Like 'Dracula's blood' for the sangria."

"I like that idea, and I think Greg and Janet will really love it," I said with a smile. This time, when Hollie grinned, it was directed at me.

She turned the page of the notebook and read over something before she spoke again. "I'm thinking to separate the two areas. What we can do is put up a curtain across the barn if that's possible."

"It's possible."

"Great!" she said as she moved in her seat some. The waitress walked up and apologized for not getting over sooner. She asked Shawn and me if we wanted something other than water, then took our drink orders, and the three of us ordered lunch.

"Okay, now for the engagement area. We want it to be a bit more romantic and lighter on the Halloween theme. I mean, if that's okay with you?"

Reaching for another scallop, I nodded. "I trust your judgment."

Hollie paused for a moment, and our eyes met. She seemed surprised, shocked even. "You do?"

I blinked a few times. "Of course, I do, Hollie. I wouldn't be sitting here if I hadn't thought you would be the one for the job."

"Oh. Um, okay. Well..."

Her voice faded off, and Shawn took that moment to speak. "Hollie, I've seen your work a dozen or more times. You are the most talented event planner in Salem. As a matter of fact, I'm going to be throwing my parents' a forty-year anniversary party, and I would love for you to help plan it."

Hollie's eyes went wide. "I'd love to!"

"Great," Shawn said. "Maybe we can meet for dinner soon."

I had to ball my fists under the table to keep from punching the shit out of my best friend. He was really going to do it. He was going to ask her out and use party planning as a shoo-in.

"I think it would be better to meet at my office. Then I can show you some anniversary parties I've done in the past."

Wait. What just happened? I looked at Shawn who was clearly attempting to not let the disappointment of being turned down show on his face.

"That will work too," he said.

"Great!" Hollie stated. "Before you leave, we'll work out a time you can swing by."

Before Shawn could say anything else, Hollie had her attention back on me. "So, I was thinking we could take a few hay bales and make a little half-circle with some blankets thrown over them."

"Okay," I said, trying not to smile like a damn fool who had just won the lottery simply because she had turned down Shawn's offer to go out. Well, to meet up and talk about a pretend anniversary party he and I both knew he wasn't going to throw.

"We'll use some hurricane lamps with maybe some rosehips in them and LED lights. I don't think your parents would want candles in the barn. Oh, speaking of, I'll use them on the candelabras as well. You won't even be able to tell they're not real."

I grinned. "Sounds great so far."

Now she smiled a full-on smile, and it made my heart want to burst from my goddamn chest. What in the living hell was happening to me?

"In the middle, I'll have a small rug with some rose petals thrown about. Edison lighting up above to give it the perfect romantic lighting. The rest will be left up to Greg. What do you think? Will Greg be on board? It's not a whole lot but is simple and romantic enough."

I sat back in the chair and looked at Hollie. She was fucking amazing, and I highly doubted she even really knew how great she was at her job.

"He's going to love it all, Hollie. I mean, you don't need me for any of this."

She laughed, and I wanted to fist-pump when I saw her cheeks stain with a bit of pink. "I will need you for moving the stuff out of storage, and since my staff will most likely be working the other parties, I'll need some help from the family with decorating. I won't be able to do it all by myself."

"Of course. They'll be there," I replied, then added in a softer voice than I had meant to use, "I'll be there to help you with whatever you need." Our eyes met and I wasn't sure how long we stared at each other before Shawn cleared his throat.

"You know, I think this is the longest the two of you have gone without fighting or issuing some kind of challenge to one another. I'm impressed. If I didn't know better, I would think you two were friends."

Before either of us could reply, the waitress brought our food. The rest of lunch was spent with Shawn talking Hollie's ear off and asking question after question about her event-planning business. Every now and then, Greg's engagement would be brought back up. Hollie asked me about the dig site. I was more than happy to talk about that and about how Shawn enjoyed being a lawyer for the city. It was actually a really pleasant lunch, and when it came time to leave, I found I wasn't ready to go. And that added to my already confused state.

After I picked up the tab, I looked at Shawn. "We should probably get going. I need to get to the office."

He gave me a shit-eating grin. "I'm not in a rush. You head on out, and I'll stay and walk Hollie to her car."

Hollie wiped the corners of her mouth and stood. "Thank you for lunch, Lucas. Thank you for the offer, Shawn, but I'm meeting my sister at my aunt's shop."

"How is the witch-crafting going? Still haven't found your inner witch yet?" I asked with a smug expression.

Hollie put her purse over her shoulder and walked up to me. Her eyes danced with amusement as she replied, "When you get the body rash that won't stop itching, then you'll know I've found her."

After she was finished speaking, she winked and walked off. I watched as I tried to remember how to breathe the right way. Damn if she wasn't spit and fire and beautiful to boot.

Shawn let out a roar of laughter. "Damn, I really like her."

I shook my head and turned back to him. "Doesn't appear the feeling is mutual."

He rolled his eyes. "She just didn't want to accept with you sitting there."

"And why would me being here have anything to do with it?"

He shrugged. "I think you forgot we drove together here. You need me to drop you off at your office or the dig site?"

Turning back to watch Hollie walk away, I had to fight the urge to follow her.

With a shake of my head, I answered, "I've got an errand to run first. I'll just walk back."

Hitting me on the shoulder, he gave me a knowing smile. "Watch out, Lucas. The wall you have up is starting to slip."

I shot him a dirty look as he laughed and then started toward his car. Once he was around the corner, I started walking toward The Covens Magick Cottage.

Chapter Three

Hollie

Kristin handed me a cup of tea, then flopped down onto the giant bean bag chair in my living room.

"He actually gave you a compliment?"

Smiling, I answered, "Yep. And he meant it. It was so weird. We didn't bicker at all. The only jabs thrown were at the very end when we were both leaving."

"Progress," she said before taking a sip of her tea. "Only took...how many years?"

Sighing, I leaned back in the chair. "Shawn was hinting at taking me out."

Her eyes went wide. "What?"

"Yep," I said as I popped my "P." "And the worst part was, Lucas wasn't even fazed by it. Like he seriously could have cared less about Shawn flirting."

Kristin leaned forward. "I told you back in high school, I thought Shawn was into you. Hell, most of Lucas's friends liked you. You know why none of them ever asked you out, don't you?"

I shook my head. "Enlighten me with your wisdom."

She shot me a smug look. "It's because they never wanted to cross that line. There has always been an imaginary line between you and Lucas. In order to stay true to their friendship with him, they never pursued you."

"An imaginary line?" I repeated.

"Yes. It's like the two of you have put up this wall that neither of you will cross. I think Lucas likes you and has for some time."

I huffed as I rolled my eyes. "That is ridiculous, Kristin."

"It's true! Larry told me."

I sat forward. Larry was one of Lucas's friends. "He told you what? Did Lucas tell them not to ask me out?"

She shook her head. "No! He never actually told any of them that. They just all assumed it. Like, one of their stupid unspoken rules. Like, you can't date your best friend's sister and crap like that. But Larry said when Lucas doesn't think people are looking, he watches you."

Tilting my head, I let her words settle in. "Watches me?"

She nodded and took a sip of her tea. "And you said today after lunch, Lucas said he was going back to his office, but you saw him outside of Lucy's store."

"Yeah, that was strange. I felt him before I saw him."

A single brow rose.

"I'm serious, Kirstin. It was weird. Why would he follow me there and then not come inside?"

Letting out an exaggerated breath, she said, "Here's a crazy idea. Have you ever thought of just telling Lucas how you feel about him?"

I was positive my eyes were as wide as saucers. "Admit I have feelings for him? No way!"

"He might react in a completely different way than what you think."

I shook my head. "He can't stand me."

"That's not true."

"Well, he certainly doesn't look at me like he likes me in that way. I mean, if I ever admitted I had feelings for him, and he told me he didn't feel the same, it would..." I exhaled and closed my eyes. "It would break my heart, Kristin. I've tried for so long to forget him. To forget that every time he walks into the same room as me, my heart feels like it skips a beat. Or my stomach does a nosedive. And the rare times he does give me that smile with his dimple, butterflies dance in my stomach. Gah! I wish I didn't feel this way about him. There have been plenty of guys I could have dated and slept with to forget about Lucas, but I'm always comparing them to him. What is wrong with me?"

"You're in love with him."

I groaned. "Stupid, stupid, heart!"

Kristin sat up and an evil grin spread on her face. "Put a spell on him."

I stared at her for a few moments before I busted out laughing. "I think you have me confused with Sarah. She's the witch."

Kristin shook her head. "Hollie, you have the power in you. I know you do."

"Have you lost your mind?" I asked. "Did you spike the tea?"

Kristin jumped up and went over to my bookshelf. She ran her fingers along the spines until she found the book she was looking for. She walked back over and held it up.

"What are you doing with our old journal?" I asked.

She started to fumble through the pages and stopped at one. "Once upon a time, you were interested in the craft, Hollie. I don't know what changed. I have an idea, but once upon a time, you believed. I think, deep down inside, you still do, and you have a gift. Use it."

"Kristin, I don't have any gifts except knowing how to throw a good party."

Shaking her head, she looked up at me. "You do things without even noticing you do them."

Frowning, I asked, "What kinds of things?"

Looking up from the journal, she said, "Answer questions before they are even asked."

I let out a humorless laugh. "I do not."

"Yes, you do. I can't tell you how many times you've done it with me, your parents, other people... At first, I thought it was just a coincidence. Then it kept happening, and one time, I was thinking of asking you if I could wear that royal blue dress of yours, and you just said, 'Of course, you can wear it.'"

Shaking my head, I replied, "You asked me if you could wear it."

"No, I asked in my head, and you answered."

I blinked a few times at her before I folded my arms over my chest. "You probably didn't realize you asked it out loud."

She rolled her eyes and looked back down at the journal. "Today is another example. You said you felt Lucas at the shop before you even saw him. What about the time I cut my hand, and I couldn't get to the phone, and you showed up at my place right before I passed out? I asked what you were doing there, and you said you had a feeling something bad had happened."

I chewed on my thumbnail. It was true. I had a weird intuition on some things. All I could do was shrug.

Kristin shook her head and kept reading until finally coming to a stop and turning the book so I could see it.

"I think this is the spell we wrote to make Johnny Harris like me. Remember?"

I laughed. "We were, like, twelve."

"Come on, let's just try it. If you truly don't believe in it, then no harm. All you want is for Lucas to just show you a bit of interest. Then you can do it from there. I do suggest you wear some shirts that show a bit more cleavage."

Shaking my head, I stood. "No."

"Oh, come on, Hollie! Why not?"

Turning to face her, I pointed to the book. "For one, most of those are made-up spells written by two twelve-year-old girls. Second, I'm not a witch. And if my memory serves me, I think we copied that spell from one of Lucy's books."

"Then let's ask Sarah to cast a spell."

"No! Besides, you cannot alter someone's free will. I know that much."

"You're not. It's a simple spell to get him to notice you." She looked down at the spell. "You know what? We did copy some of these out of that black spell book your aunt told you not to ever touch."

Sighing, I headed into the kitchen and grabbed a bottle of wine. "All the more reason I'm not doing it, Kristin."

She crossed her arms over her chest and asked, "Are you afraid?"

I stopped and slowly turned to face her. "Excuse me?"

She gasped. "You are. You're totally afraid it will work. You're afraid that Lucas will notice you."

Narrowing my eyes at her, I clenched my jaw tightly as I slowly replied, "I am not afraid. I am, however, not going to put a spell on a guy to like me if he can't like me on his own. I want to know that the feelings between us are true."

"So, you do believe in witchcraft!"

With a frustrated growl, I started toward the kitchen.

"That's it, isn't it? All those years you were teased for your family's witchcraft history has made you afraid to admit that you just might have the gift."

Turning to face my best friend, I drew in a slow breath and then lied, "I'm not afraid."

With one of her perfectly arched brows raised, she said, "Prove it."

Three hours later

Three bottles of wine and two shots of tequila between the two of us later, I found myself sitting in the middle of my living room, faux spell book in hand with an altar set up on the floor.

Kristin sat down next to me. "Okay, we've got his picture. Put it in the middle."

I placed a picture of Lucas in the middle of the salt circle I'd made on the floor. We had cut the picture out of my yearbook, which I would regret in the morning when I was sober.

"I think we have to use a certain color candle," I said, impressed that I wasn't slurring and that I could somewhat remember how all this worked.

Kristin held up two candles. "All you have is red and black."

Tapping my finger on my chin, I pointed to the black one. "That one."

Frowning, Kristin said, "I think we should use red."

"No!" I shouted. "Red is for passion. Love! Desire. I just want him to notice me, not fall in love with me."

"But you said you can't alter free will."

I shrugged and hiccupped before I said, "Better to play it safe."

We both nodded.

I giggled when I read the title of the spell. "To make a man fall..."

Looking up at her, I frowned. "We never finished writing the name of the spell. How do we know this is the right one?"

"I'm, like, 95 percent sure that is the right spell."

"Good odds."

She nodded.

Clearing my throat, I picked up the white sage and lavender smudge stick that we had lit earlier and moved it around, letting the smoke and scent fill the air as I read. I'd need to fill in the rest of the title of the spell since I wasn't sure what it really was.

"To Make a Man Fall...for you!"

Kristin giggled.

I used my best spell-making voice as I said, "You need an eye of newt."

Kristin handed me a mustard bottle. "I couldn't find any mustard seeds in your pantry."

"It will have to do." I put a few drops around Lucas's picture as we both giggled.

"Um, next is toadstool powder!"

Baby powder and a mushroom appeared in my hand. I sprinkled the powder over the picture, then put the mushroom on it.

"Wing of bat!" I called out and dropped a bat that I had hanging up on my wall as part of my Halloween decorations.

"Hair of man." I looked up at her. "I don't have a piece of his hair."

She grinned. "Yes, you do! Remember in second grade, when you put bubble gum in his hair, and your mom had to cut it out? You saved it!"

I was about to argue with her that I hadn't kept it but decided it wasn't worth it. She knew everything about me. I stood up, swayed slightly, and then pointed to her. "You're right! Be right back!"

Racing up the steps, I couldn't help but wonder, even in my drunken state, if it was a little bit weird that I had kept his hair all those years.

After searching through a box of stuff from high school, I found the baggy with Lucas's hair in it. I raced back downstairs, slipping and taking the last three steps on my ass. I rushed into the living room and held up the bag.

"His hair!"

Kristin grabbed the bag and opened it, pulling a few small strands out and putting them in my hand. I drew in a breath and dropped them on our pile.

"What next?" she asked.

"Um...spirit of a raven."

We both looked at each other before Kristin lit up. "Here, let's use this!"

She grabbed a piece of black licorice and handed it to me. I held it up and said, "I declare you to be the spirit of a raven!"

The fire in the fireplace popped, and we both screamed, then fell into another fit of laughter.

"Not a witch, my ass!" Kristin cackled.

I tossed it onto the pile as we both fell into a fit of laughter.

"Next is...ew, gross. It's snake venom and spider legs!"

Kristin screwed up her face.

"I have an idea!" I got up and walked outside, returning with a rubber snake and spider I got off one of the displays on my porch and held them up.

"*Voila!* Problem solved."

Kristin pointed to me. "Oh, my God, you're so smart."

I dropped down to the floor and held up the decorations. "I declare you the venom-filled snake thing, and you, spider legs!" I tossed them onto the pile, and a crack of thunder from outside rattled the house.

Kristin crinkled her nose. "Was it supposed to storm?"

"Don't you know?" I asked with a laugh. "I'm a witch!"

"Okay, but what does the thunder outside have to do with that?"

"I don't know!" I said as I started to laugh, which made her laugh.

We laughed so hard, I had tears sliding down my face. It took a good ten minutes before I could regain control.

"Okay, back to the spell!"

"Right. Right. Okay.... It says to... Let's see. Mash it, crunch it, mix it all together. Say his name three times and put him in sunder. I'm not putting my hand in the mustard, so we'll just do this."

Picking up the black candle, I tipped it and held it over the pile so it could drip onto it all.

"Lucas Dayton. Lucas Dayton. Lucas Dayton. I put you in sunder! And so it is, the spell is cast. So mote it be."

I blew out the candle and looked at Kristin who handed me a glass of wine.

"Cheers to getting Lucas to fall for you."

We clinked glasses, and I downed my drink.

The loud knocking at my front door jerked me up into a sitting position. My head was throbbing, and my stomach instantly rolled.

"Oh, dear God, how much did I drink?"

A quick glance around the room told me I had most likely drunk a lot. Every single light was on, and Frank Sinatra's "Witchcraft" was playing on my phone and appeared to be on repeat.

Kristin was curled up into a ball on the large bean bag chair, clutching a book in her arms.

Another knock, followed by the doorbell.

Slowly pulling myself up, I stumbled to the door and opened it to find my sister standing there.

"Sarah, why are you here so early?" I asked.

She took one look at me, and her eyes went wide.

"What did you do, Hollie?"

I motioned for her to come in. "I apparently drank too much."

Sarah whisked past me, leaving me slightly dizzy.

"Did you happen to bring coffee? Did I see coffee in your hand?" I asked as I followed her.

"Oh, no. I knew it! You used magick last night!"

I turned and got a better view of the living room. In the middle of the floor was a circle of white. God, I hoped that wasn't sugar. In the middle of the circle was a bunch of junk. As I walked closer, I saw a picture of Lucas with what looked to be candle wax dripped on it. My heart dropped to my stomach as it all started to come back to me.

Kristin sat up and yawned, the spell book falling to the floor. "Okay, how did you know she used magick? Is that like a witch thing or a sister thing?"

Sarah ignored Kristin, picked up the book, and opened it to the page Kristin had marked. She gasped and looked at the floor, then at me.

"You cast a spell, Hollie!"

I laughed, then quickly stopped when my head demanded I do so and fast.

"We were playing around with a silly little spell we made up when we were little."

Sarah shook her head as she looked through the book, then bent down and moved the items around. She picked up the picture of Lucas and then stood up and glared at me. "Which spell did you use?"

Kristin stood and pointed to the spell that was on the page she had marked. "Don't get your panties into a wad, Sarah. It was a little notice-me spell, that's all."

Sarah's eyes narrowed. "You did this spell?"

"Apparently," I said as I made my way to the sofa. "I need aspirin."

"I'll go get some," Kristin said as she walked out of the living room.

"Are you sure this is the spell you did, Hollie?" Sarah asked, this time in a softer, quieter voice.

"Um...I don't know. Something with bat wings and eye newts and spider legs. We never finished writing the title...so I filled it in. I think we copied the spell?"

"I told you, we wrote them from one of your aunt's spell books," Kristin called out from the bathroom. "Hollie filled it in and said to make him fall for her, or something like that."

Sarah showed me the spell. "To Make Him Fall in Sunder?"

I shook my head. "No, I think it was, like, to make him fall under my charms or something like that."

"No, Hollie. It is to make him fall in sunder."

Frowning, I said, "Sunder? Yeah, I think that word was in there."

Sarah closed her eyes. "Hollie, look at this spell. Was this it?"

"Jesus, Sarah, what difference does it make? It was all in fun."

"Look at it!" she cried. I felt the urgency in her voice and walked over to her. After I read the unfinished title and the first two lines, I nodded. "Yes, that's it. I filled in the title."

Slowly shaking her head, I could see the disappointment on my sister's face. I knew how seriously she took the craft, and I felt guilty for making it seem like it was nothing.

"You put a hex on him, Hollie. You put a hex on Lucas."

I laughed. "A hex? Sarah, listen to yourself. I mean, we didn't even use the right things. I mean...I used mustard and decorations. We were drunk and just messing around."

She sighed. "Hollie, it doesn't matter. If you cast the spell, and you truly believed at the time that you were casting it, then you put a spell on Lucas. And not a spell to make him fall under your charm. A bad spell! The full title of this spell is To Make a Man Fall a Sunder."

That caught my attention. "Bad spell?"

"Yes! You copied this out of the spell book Lucy told you to stay out of, didn't you?" Sarah asked.

At about that time, Kristin walked in and handed me a bottle of water and a few Tylenol. "We copied the spell out of a book that was at the store. It was a big black book that she kept in her office. We were in there doing homework and got bored. I remember Hollie said it was a secret spell book and that Lucy never wanted her to open it."

"How do you remember this stuff?" I asked as I took the Tylenol from her.

Kristin shrugged. "I don't know. I have a really good memory."

"Because it's one of your gifts," Sarah said before she looked back at me with worried eyes.

"It's fine. So what if we copied it down? We didn't even use the right things. I used a rubber spider!"

Closing her eyes, Sarah shook her head. "She never let us see it because they aren't spells, they're cures. You cast a hex on Lucas."

Kristin laughed this time. "Sarah, I totally get that you're heavy into this, but do you see what is in the pile? Those are Halloween decorations!"

I finished off my water. "That's what I told her."

Sarah reached down and picked up the black candle. "You would have used red, not black."

"She didn't want him to fall in love with her," Kristin explained helpfully.

"You cannot alter someone's free will, but you can give them passion," Sarah stated.

Kristin turned to me. "Maybe you are a witch. She sounds just like you."

Sarah sighed. "Black is used for protection, repelling, banishing."

I froze. "Repelling?"

Slowly shaking her head, she handed me the candle and the book. "You got yourself into this, Hollie Craft, you're going to have to get yourself out of it."

I stared down at the book, then snapped my head up to watch my sister walk toward the front door.

"Sarah, how in the world did you know we were messing around last night?"

With her hand on the doorknob, she looked over her shoulder. "I felt the magick coming from you."

My entire body shivered. "You *felt* the magick?" I asked, trying to sound as if I thought she was insane.

"Yes, Hollie. You may not want to believe it's true, but you are indeed a witch, whether you want to believe it or not."

Before I could say a word, she was out the door, and I jumped when it slammed shut.

I turned to look at Kristin. "You don't think we...?"

She laughed, but it wasn't very convincing. "No way. Not in a million years. Although, the whole fire cracking and thunder thing was kind of weird."

Nodding, I looked back down at the circle on the floor and tried to ignore the strange sensation that coursed through my entire body.

"You don't really think you actually put a hex on him, do you?" Kristin asked as I stared at the picture of Lucas.

"No, no. It was all in fun, that's all," I said, not sure who I was trying to convince. I looked over at Kristin and forced a smile. "It was silly, and we were drunk. I had no idea what I was even doing."

She nodded and returned my smile. But there was something in my best friend's eyes that told me she wasn't convinced either.

"Well, time will tell. Right?"

I swallowed hard. "Time will tell."

Sitting down on the sofa, I stared down at the picture of Lucas.

"What do you think your sister meant when she said a good memory was one of my gifts?"

Swallowing hard, I looked at my best friend. "I think we both know what she was saying."

Kristin bit down on her lip. I didn't need for Kristin to say what she was thinking. I heard it loud and clear.

"If two witches cast a spell, it makes the spell that much stronger."

Our gazes locked, and Kristin whispered, "We're so badass."

Chapter Four

Lucas

City archaeologist. That was my job. I also carried the title of historical preservation officer for the city of Salem, Massachusetts. And I loved my job, usually. But right now, all I wanted to do was crawl back into bed and go to sleep. Nothing had been going right since I'd woken up. It had been a series of accidents since I stepped out of bed.

I stubbed my toe on a chair. Spilled coffee on my shirt. Nearly fell down the steps of my back porch and broke my neck, and now, I was being called out to the field. And for some reason, it was the last place I wanted to be. I normally loved being out in the field, so I wasn't sure why it was bothering me today.

Anyone who knew me knew history was something I was passionate about. So, after doing an internship during high school with the then-city archaeologist, Mary Sinclair, I knew that was the job I wanted. The fact that Mary retired and the city hired me to replace her was a bonus.

One of my favorite archaeology sites was the home of Samuel Parris. Anyone familiar with the Salem witch trials knows that it all started there. The site was open to visitors now, but we were doing another dig not far from the home. We had stumbled upon it by mistake. The city was getting ready to excavate for a park, and artifacts were found, causing the park project to be put on hold. Now we had the city breathing down our backs to hurry up and get all the historical items out of the area so they could continue with their project.

As I ducked under the rope keeping the site blocked off, I tripped and caught myself with my hands. My pants, unfortunately, caught on something and ripped. I stood and cursed as a shooting pain hit the middle of my hand.

"Son of..."

"You're bleeding!" a woman said from in front of me. I looked up to see Lori Sinclair, Mary's daughter.

I glanced down to see my hand was cut. "Shit," I mumbled.

"Here, let me."

Zipping open the little pack she had around her waist, she pulled out a wipe and a band-aid.

"You don't have to do that, Lori," I said as I attempted to pull my hand out of hers. The woman was stronger than I would have imagined and kept her grip on my hand while she cleaned it and put a band-aid on it.

"You might need to get a bandage on it if it doesn't stop bleeding," she said with a smile.

Manny Hawks, one of the archeologists assigned to the dig, made his way over to me, calling out my name. He looked at Lori, then at me.

"What happened, boss?" he asked, a knowing smirk on his face.

"Nothing, I tripped and cut my hand."

Lori looked up at me with those big doe eyes of hers and smiled. "All set, Lucas."

"Um, thanks, Lori."

46

"Sure. I'll be over there, cataloging things."

I nodded. "Great. Thanks."

With another look down at my hand and then up at me, she blushed and turned to walk away.

Once she was out of earshot, I faced Manny. "Don't even say it."

"Dude, she wants you."

I rolled my eyes. "How are things going?"

"How are they going? We found out what building was here, or at least, I think we're on the right path with the items we've been recovering."

My eyes went wide, and I could feel my heartbeat picking up. I loved that moment when we made a discovery.

"What?" I asked, my breath nearly crackling with anticipation.

"A tavern."

"A tavern?" I repeated as I looked at the massive area that we were working on. No matter where you were in New England, if you dug, you were sure to find something, but a tavern that wasn't ever recorded to be in that spot—now that was interesting. "I wasn't aware there was a tavern in this area."

"No one was," Manny said as he stepped over another rope. "Look at that well, Lucas. Look at it!"

I smiled. The large well was lined with rocks and was in unbelievably good condition.

"You found a well. A rather intact well, but what makes you think this site was a tavern?"

Manny motioned for me to follow him. "We found this earlier this morning."

I stopped at the table where four people sat, including Lori. They were to document anything we found. Sitting on the table were two old beer mugs, three teacups, and what looked to be a smoking pipe. A perfectly intact smoking pipe.

Up until this morning, we had found only pieces of pottery, two teacups, and some kitchen items.

I reached down and picked up the mug. "Holy shit."

Manny laughed. "Can you imagine what we're going to find, Lucas?"

I shook my head. "I need to go and change."

Another roar of laughter from my work colleague and friend. "It's time to dig in the dirt, my friend. We finally found the pot of gold. It has to be a tavern, with those types of items."

Hitting him on the back, I smiled. "Good job, Manny. Good job."

"Go do what you need to do because I know you, Lucas. You're gonna want to be here when we dig up more stuff."

I nodded and turned to head back to my car.

That had been what I needed to turn my day around. What started out as a bad day looked now to be turning out to be a great day.

At least, that was what I thought.

The door to my hospital room flew open, and I jerked my head up to see Hollie Craft standing there, a look of horror on her face.

"What happened?" she asked as she made her way over to the side of the bed.

"Ahh...I was getting out of my car and started across the parking lot, and some idiot hit me."

Her hand went to her mouth, and she gasped.

"It's okay, Hollie. I'm fine. Nothing is broken, but I do have some bruised ribs. The doctor wants me to go home and rest for a few days. The problem is, we think we found a possible tavern at the dig site. I need to get back to it. I can't go home and rest."

She swallowed hard. "So, it was an accident?"

I felt my brows pull down. "Yes. Unless you paid someone to try and run me over, and you're here to see why he failed."

Her face drained of color. "What!? Oh, my God, I would never do that. I would never try and hurt you!"

I reached for her hand and gave it a squeeze. "Hollie, I was kidding. I thought it would be funny, you know, because of our past and everything."

There was a knock at the door, and Wendy poked her head in. Shit. Greg must have told Janet, and she told Wendy.

"Lucas!" she cried out, rushing to the other side of the bed. She leaned down and went to kiss me. Thank God my reflexes were good because I turned my head, and she got the side of my face, damn near my ear, instead of the full-on mouth kiss she had wanted.

"Wendy, what are you doing here?" I asked.

"Janet told me what happened! Greg said you've had a terrible day altogether."

"What?" Hollie asked, concern in her voice. It was then Wendy looked at her, and by the expression on her face, she wasn't pleased to see another woman standing in my hospital room, especially Hollie. I wasn't sure what it was about Hollie that Wendy didn't like, but she never made it a secret that she didn't care for her.

"Hollie, what are you doing here? You hate Lucas."

Hollie's eyes went wide with shock. "I don't hate him."

"Really?" Wendy asked with a laugh. "You certainly don't like him."

"That is not true, Wendy," Hollie said as she put her hands on her hips. "Why would you even say that?"

Wendy tilted her head and stared at Hollie. "Oh, I don't know... All the times you've fought with him. Said mean things to him. I'm surprised it wasn't you behind the wheel of that car!"

"Wendy!" I said in a stern voice that reminded me of my father, ignoring the shooting pain in my side.

"What did you say?" Hollie said in a voice so low and frightening, Wendy took a step away. I couldn't blame her. I would have, too, if I had the ability to stand at that moment. Hollie looked ready to tear Wendy apart. "Did you really just accuse me of what I think you did?"

Wendy blinked a few times. "I... I... Well, I... I mean, you are...um...kind of mean and..."

Hollie and I both waited to see how Wendy was going to get herself out the word-vomit she had just made.

When Wendy's cell phone rang, she let out a nervous laugh. "Saved by the phone. I've got to run to work. I'll call you later, sweetie!"

Wendy answered her phone and rushed out the door. Hollie followed her with her eyes, and when the door shut, she whispered, "I hope you get a rash all over your body."

I laughed. "Now, *that* was mean."

Hollie whipped her head back around and looked at me. "Are you two dating again?"

"What? No. We've never really dated. We've just..."

Nice, Lucas. You almost just told the woman you've been pining over since you were in middle school that you had a fuck buddy.

"We're just friends, that's all."

Hollie forced a tight smile. "What did she mean when she said you've had a bad day?"

I sighed and pushed my hand through my hair. I couldn't help but notice how Hollie's nose flared slightly, and her eyes seemed to turn darker as she watched my hand.

"It started off as a bad day. I stubbed my toe, spilled hot coffee on myself." I held up my hand. The nurse had replaced the band-aid with a white bandage after she insisted I could have cut it on something rusty and old. "Cut my hand at the dig site."

Her hand came back up to her mouth, and she looked panicked.

"I thought the day was getting better. We found what looks to be an old tavern site just down from the Parris home. I was on my way home to change so I could help at the site but swung by the office first to take care of some emails. I was walking in the parking lot when I got hit. Jerk was speeding."

Hollie dropped her hand, then dropped into the seat that was next to the bed. All the color drained from her face as she stared at me.

"Hey, are you okay?" I asked when she started to breathe harder.

"When did the bad luck start?"

I frowned. "The bad luck?"

Nodding, she motioned with her hands for me to hurry up. "Yes, Lucas. When did it start?"

"Today? I mean, yesterday, I twisted my ankle on a run, but that wasn't anything. Oh, if you want to call this bad luck, my plumbing got backed up, and I had to call someone to fix it. I also burned my dinner last night, which is crazy because I've never done that in my entire life. Almost set the stove on fire."

"Oh, God. Oh, God. Oh, God."

She kept chanting and rocking in the chair while she waved her hands like she was hot.

"Hollie, what's wrong? Why are you even here? How did you know I was hurt? Greg? My mom?"

Her head snapped up, and our eyes met. "I felt it," she whispered.

"You...felt it?" I asked in confusion. "How did you *feel* me getting hurt?"

With a confused expression, she slowly shook her head. "I don't know how to explain, Lucas. I got a feeling something bad happened to you. I called your office to talk to you, and they said the ambulance had just taken you to the hospital, that there had been an accident."

I raised my brows. "So, you're saying when I got hit, you felt it?"

Her upper teeth dug into her lower lip, and I nearly groaned at the erotic thoughts that filled my head. I had to adjust on the bed so she wouldn't see my dick grow harder.

"I'm not sure. I think so," she finally said before she stood up so fast, she nearly knocked the chair over. "I have to go."

"Hollie! Wait!" I cried out, then winced as a pain shot up my left side. She rushed out the door just as my mother was walking in.

"What in the world did you say to Hollie to make her run out of here like that, Lucas Dayton?"

Staring at the door Hollie had run out of, I said, "I have no idea."

Chapter Five

Hollie

I rushed into Aunt Lucy's store and stopped when I saw her talking to someone. She glanced up and smiled at me.

"Hollie, I've been expecting you."

Oh, Lord, what did that mean?

"What are you going here?" Sarah asked from my left. I spun to face her.

"You were right."

One brow slowly raised as if to say she was always right. "About what?"

I glanced back to the couple Lucy was talking to, then grabbed my sister by the arm and dragged her into the other room of Lucy's store. The room where she kept all the potions, crystals, and spell-type stuff.

When I was positive no one would hear, I drew in a deep breath, then closed my eyes as I exhaled and said, "I can't believe I'm about to say this."

"Say what?"

Looking at my sister, I leaned in closer and whispered, "I

think the spell I put on Lucas worked. I mean, it didn't work the way I wanted it to work because I used the wrong spell."

"You put a hex on him," Sarah said, folding her arms across her chest.

"Did you tell Aunt Lucy?"

Sarah frowned. "No. I told you, you're going to have to clean this up yourself."

I shook my head in confusion. "But when I walked in, she said she was expecting me."

Sighing, Sarah gave me a pitying look, like I should know why my aunt said that. "She probably felt you doing magick, like I did."

Feeling frustrated, I spat out, "That is the most ridiculous thing you've ever said. How in the hell would you feel that?"

"How did you know Lucas was hurt?"

My mouth opened to reply, but I quickly snapped it shut. "How did you know that?"

"I'm a witch." Then she flashed a shit-eating grin. "And Rose called. She said you told Lucas you felt he had gotten hurt and that he said you were acting very strange at the hospital. She wanted to make sure you were okay."

I started to wring my hands. "Did she also tell you he's had a series of misfortunes all day? And that they started yesterday? Yesterday, Sarah. The day after I put the spell..." She tilted her head. "The hex, the day after I put the hex on him."

"That, she did not tell me. What kinds of misfortunes?"

I started to pace back and forth. "I don't know. He stubbed his toes, spilled hot coffee on himself, cut his hand, burned his dinner, nearly started a fire in his stove, got into a car accident...! I mean, do I really need to go on? No one has that kind of bad luck all at once."

My aunt's voice came from behind me. "This is what happens when you try to do magick and think it's all a game."

Spinning around, I watched as my aunt drew near me.

She tsked as she stopped in front of me. "This isn't a game, Hollie. You've ignored this for far too long. The gift is powerful in you—we all saw it when you were little. You're probably a better witch than me, your mother, and Sarah put together."

"Mom doesn't think she's a witch," I reminded my aunt. But the moment the words were out of my mouth, I somehow knew they weren't true.

She smiled. "Your mother tells you that, my dear. She's never wanted you to feel like you were out of sorts since you hadn't fully come to believe in your powers. It was hard enough on you in school with the kids teasing you."

I turned to Sarah and gave her a questioning look. She nodded. "You've never wondered why Mom is fascinated with all her herbs and her garden? Or how she has so many crystals she collects? Come on, Hollie, you cannot be that naïve. You chose to ignore it because you wanted to be normal."

I felt dizzy and stumbled back. Suddenly, a stool was there to catch my fall. I couldn't help but notice the look between my aunt and sister. Almost as if they were proud.

"Thank you, Aunt Lucy."

"For?" she asked.

"The stool."

Lucy moved across the small room swiftly, her long, black skirt trailing behind her. She stood next to Sarah. Both of them were dressed in black. Lucy wore a skirt and a black dress shirt. Sarah wore a really cute black knee-length dress, paired with a touch of red on the neckline of her long cardigan sweater.

"Do you always wear black to the store?" I asked randomly. They both ignored me.

"I didn't move the stool for you," Lucy stated.

I looked at my sister, who shook her head.

A bubble of laughter came out. "What, next you're going to tell me I moved it?"

"If the broomstick fits," Sarah said with a smirk.

"You guys, I didn't move the stool." I stood and turned to face the stool. "If I moved it, then let it move back to where it was."

When the stool slid across the floor to the table, I covered my mouth with both hands and cried out, "Holy fuck!"

"This is why you shouldn't be practicing the craft, Hollie. And you should never put a hex on someone. Our craft is about manifestation, protection, harmony, clearing... balance."

I waved my hand in front of me. "Yes, yes, I know all of that. But you mean to tell me you've never put a spell on someone to...to...?"

They both leaned forward.

"To what, dear?"

"Make him notice you!" I cried out.

The bell on the front door chimed, and Sarah made her way out of the small room to greet the shoppers.

My aunt's store was adorable. It wasn't like some of the other "witch" stores in Salem. She sold a lot of products for self-care that she, Sarah, and my mother all made themselves. She also sold paper goods, art, and Salem-touristy things. But then there was the area of the store for people who practiced witchcraft. Things like potions, tarot and oracle decks, candles, and other wares a witch might need.

I'll admit, I once bought her heart-mender potion when Lucas asked another girl to prom. Someone should have told me it would only mend my heart for, like, two days.

"If you needed help getting someone to notice you, you could have come to me. I would have helped you. Instead, you got drunk, used a spell you had no business using, and made a joke of it all. And look at what happened."

"So, you think it was me? I'm the reason Lucas was hit by that car?"

"The important question here, Hollie, is do you believe it was you?"

I instantly started to chew on my thumbnail.

The door chimed again, and I heard Sarah greeting someone.

"Hi, Wendy! It's so nice to see you."

I rolled my eyes, and my hand took my other hand and gave it a squeeze. As much as I tried to forget all the mean things Wendy Hoffman had said to me when I was younger, it was hard to do. Especially when she had gotten her claws into Lucas.

"Hi, Sarah. I need some kind of lotion or bath salt for this rash that just appeared within the last hour."

Gasping, I turned to face Lucy.

I mouthed, *Oh, my God*. Then started pointing to myself.

"Use your words, dear. I don't read minds—that wasn't one of my gifts."

Grabbing my aunt by the arm, I pulled her further into the room and away from Sarah and Wendy. "I did that! Holy shit. Holy shit. Holy shit. When she left the hospital, I said I hoped she got a rash!"

"My goodness. Just think, if you honed in on that gift, how amazing you would be. Doing good, I mean. Right now, it seems you're a little rusty."

Spinning around on my heels, I made my way out to the main part of the store. Sarah was showing Wendy some products. I casually made my way closer to them.

"Oh, hey, Wendy. Fancy seeing you here."

Wendy jumped and took a few steps away from me. My mouth fell open, and I couldn't help but stare at the rash that was all over her face and neck.

She shot me a dirty look. "Hollie."

"So, did you really mean that at the hospital when you said you were surprised that I wasn't the one driving the car that hit Lucas?"

Sarah's eyes nearly bugged out of her head as she looked at Wendy, then back to me. She pointed to her and mouthed, *Did you do this?*

I smiled a triumphant smile.

"Of course not, Hollie. I was upset. As you know, Lucas and I are very, *very* close."

"Is that so?" I asked, feeling jealousy about to rear her ugly head. "I asked if you were dating, and he said no. That you're just friends."

She jerked as if I had just slapped her. Then a slow smile crossed her face as she tilted her head and replied, "With benefits, if you catch my meaning."

I really don't like this woman.

I was about to wish some hemorrhoids on her when Sarah cleared her throat.

I gave a one-shoulder shrug. "I didn't get that vibe from him. Anyway, I hope you..." I used my finger to motion to her face and neck. "...get that cleared up soon. Looks bad."

"Hollie, may I speak with you?" Lucy asked from across the room.

Flashing Wendy the fakest smile I could muster, I followed my aunt into her small office at the back of her store.

The faint sound of the door clicking had me turning to face her.

"Looks like you summoned your powers, dear. Now, what are you going to do about it?"

I sat down in the seat opposite her desk. I might have not been a believer in all this hocus pocus stuff yesterday, but today...today was starting to change my mindset. Maybe deep down inside, I always knew it was true. Sarah was right. I had started to push the idea away once the teasing in school started. It sucked coming from a family of witches while living in Salem.

"Today, I had this feeling come over me that Lucas had been hurt. I tried to ignore it but decided to call his office. That's when I found out he had been hit by a car. Is that a power I possess?"

Lucy leaned against the table that was behind her desk and smiled at me. She looked so much like my mother, just a bit younger.

"Yes, that is."

"Oy vey." I stood and paced before I dropped back down in the chair. "I'm not, unfortunately."

"You're not what?"

"You just asked me if I was free for dinner tonight. I'm not."

The corner of Lucy's mouth twitched. "I didn't voice my question, Hollie. You heard it and answered. You've been able to do that since you were about five. Respond to questions before they were even asked."

I blinked at her a few times. "Kristin said the same thing to me the other day. I don't think I do that."

She chuckled. "Ask anyone who knows you, Hollie. You don't do it often. I think your mind is far too busy, but when it is settled, you can sense things. When you started school, you would answer the teacher's questions before she even asked them. That was when those awful little girls started to tease you. From that point on, you started to push your powers slowly away. You've always been able to sense things, so I'm not surprised that when Lucas was hurt, you felt it."

"Sense things?"

Nodding, Lucy said, "One time, when you were seven, you came running into the house to tell us that Nathan had fallen off the swing and broken something. Your mother and father panicked and ran outside. The second they were in view of the swing set, they saw Nathan fall to the ground. He broke his wrist trying to catch himself. You saw it before it even happened. Your mother was in shock. We've never had someone in the family that possessed the powers you have. Well, we have, but it's been a long time. She thought it was too powerful for a child. So, that was when she decided to pretend like she didn't believe in the craft in the hope that you would as well."

"What?" I softly asked as I searched my brain for the memory. "I don't remember that."

"That doesn't surprise me."

"But I can see having that happen with Nathan. He's my brother. Why Lucas?"

"You have a strong connection to Lucas Payton."

I laughed. "Hardly, Lucy. We can barely stand to be around one another."

She tilted her head and gave me a look that said I was spewing bullshit.

"Fine. I secretly like him, but that doesn't mean we have a connection."

Walking around the table, she walked over to another table, picked up her cards, and walked back to the desk.

"I don't think you needed a spell to gain Lucas's attention, Hollie," she said as she started to turn them over and place them on her desk. "As a matter of fact, I think by you using the wrong spell, for the wrong reason, you countered it."

"It wasn't a hex?"

"It was a spell to put a man in sunder, yes. The spell was meant to cause harm, but your true feelings for Lucas were mixed in with the spell. You truly didn't want to cause him harm, you wanted his attention. Throw in the fact that you were casting the spell in all the wrong ways, and it turned out to be something different."

"A bad luck spell?"

She pointed to me. "Yes. Now, you need to fix it."

I leaned forward, eager to hear what she was going to do. "What are you going to do?"

Laughing, she shook her head. "Not me, *you*. You need to fix it. You cast the original spell, Hollie."

Dropping back into the chair, I cursed under my breath. "Shit."

"The question is, do you want to break the spell off of him?"

"Yes! He got hit by a car, for Pete's sake. What do I have to do?"

Lucy cleared her throat and moved behind her desk. "You'll need to ward off negative energy."

I nodded. "Ward off negative energy. Should I be writing this down?"

Suddenly a pen and paper appeared in front of me. My eyes lifted from the paper to my aunt's knowing gaze.

"You've just never noticed it before, dear, but I've been doing magick around you since you were born. We believe what we truly want to see."

Clearing my throat, I grabbed the pen and started to write.

"Okay, I've got to ward off negative energy."

"You'll need to invite good luck and good fortune."

Writing it all down, I looked up. "How do I do that?"

"You'll need..." She turned to her table and reached for something. "...one green candle."

She set the candle down in front of me.

"One tablespoon of cinnamon powder."

She placed a small bag next to the candle.

"And salt."

"Salt?" I asked. "What is it with the salt?"

Lucy gave me a warning look.

"Sorry, go on."

She nodded.

"You're going to put the green candle on the center of your altar."

"Got it. Is a regular table okay?"

"Yes, a regular table is okay."

Was that a touch of amusement in her voice?

"Spread some salt around the candle to protect it."

I chewed on my lower lip as I wrote. "Okay, got it."

"Then you'll take a deep breath. Exhale. Have Lucas do the same. Then have him say, 'Bad luck, I command you to leave me right now.'"

Looking up in horror, I asked, "He has to say it? He has to be there?"

She nodded. "Then after he says it, you'll light the green candle. Have him take a moment to visualize how the bad luck has been affecting him. This is important."

"Fuck me," I whispered.

Ignoring me, she went on. "After he does that, he has to repeat the words, 'All adversity now dissolves.'"

I shook my head and dropped the pen. It would never work. How in the heck would I ever talk Lucas into doing this? He would think I was crazy. "Can't I do this without Lucas?"

"No."

Her answer was clipped.

My hand went to my stomach in an attempt to calm the sick feeling. "What next?" I softly asked.

"Have him close his eyes and visualize an empty canvas. Tell him to fill that canvas with whatever he would like to attract. He can look at it as a new beginning. A fresh start. It's important he takes his time with this part."

I swallowed hard. He was going to have me committed and would most likely laugh while they dragged me away in a straight jacket. I'd have to remind him I was the only person who could make his brother's proposal amazing.

"Next, have him open his eyes and sprinkle cinnamon over the circle of salt. Cinnamon helps manifest positive change. A very powerful spice, in many ways."

I nodded.

"Then he has to say, 'Only good luck and positive energy flows to me now.'"

Quickly writing it down, I looked up at my aunt. "What else?"

"That's it. You'll want him to meditate for a few minutes. Have him visualize that new beginning."

All I could do was nod as I looked down at the green candle.

"It is important the candle burn all the way down, Hollie. Very important."

"Okay. What if he has to leave?"

"He can burn it again the next day, but he must burn the entire candle. Once it is done, bury it in fresh soil."

"There isn't any other way I can do this? Like, some potion or pill I can give him?"

"Well," she said with a tilt of her head, "you could get a soap."

"A soap! Yes, I like where this is going."

"And have him sit in a bath as hot as he can stand it. Then you must cleanse his entire body while you have a smudge stick of blue sage and sunflowers burning in the same room."

Blinking several times at her, I asked, "I'm sorry, did you say I had to bathe him?"

She nodded. "You are the one who cast the spell on him. You would need to remove it."

"Is he...naked?"

She laughed. "Well do you get into a bath with clothes on? The blue sage cleanses away negativity, and sunflower brings happiness, wishes, and wisdom."

I quickly wrote that down. "Do you have any here in the store?"

"I do. Let me go get you one."

Lucy got up and left her office. I read over the spell, then read over it again.

"Okay, so my two options are to give him a bath or get him to do this little spell." I shrugged. "I mean, he might like the idea of the bath but probably from someone like Wendy."

It wasn't lost on me that I said her name like a jealous teenager.

The door to Lucy's office opened, and she walked in. She set the smudge stick down next to the other items. "And here is the soap in case you want to go that route."

I picked up the soap and inhaled. It smelled heavenly.

After gathering everything up and putting it in a basket Lucy gave me, I said my goodbyes to her and my sister and left. I needed a plan, and a good plan at that.

What I didn't hear when I was walking away was my sister asking my aunt why she hadn't simply given me the potion for Lucas to take. And my aunt's reply of, "What fun would that be?"

Chapter Six

Hollie

I drew in a deep breath before I placed my hand on the doorknob and turned it. The moment I stepped inside, I froze. Lucas was standing there with his shirt off and holding it in his hand. My eyes quickly took in his fit form and perfect, washboard abs.

"Um, what are you doing?" I asked.

"Shut the door, will you? Then will you help me get this shirt on?"

Clearing my throat, I walked in and shut the door before I made my way closer to him but not too close.

"What did you need? Where are your bandages? I thought you hurt your ribs."

"Bruised them, and they don't wrap them up. Here, can you help me get this on?"

Lucas handed me his shirt, and I took it without even thinking. The smell of pine and something earthy assaulted my senses. I had to fight the urge to walk up and sniff the man.

"You want me to help you get dressed?" I asked, my voice sounding a little too high-pitched.

He chuckled. "Just the upper half of me. The nurse helped with my pants and shoes, but she had to leave to help another nurse."

"Are you going home?" I asked.

"Yes." His eyes looked down at the shirt in my hands. "Do you mind helping?"

I jumped into action and placed the basket I had been carrying on the bed. "Of course, I'm sorry. I was just shocked to walk in and see you without a shirt on."

"Virgin eyes can't take it?"

I huffed and tried to act like his words hadn't nearly had me asking him how he knew I was still a virgin.

Yes, I'm still a virgin. Sue me for wanting to save myself for the right man.

Attempting to keep my hands from shaking, I carefully helped him get his shirt on. He hissed once when he had to move his arm and then twisted his body to get his arm in the sleeve. Moving to stand in front of him, I started to button it up. I could feel the heat of his eyes on me and was wondering where that gift was my aunt was talking about. I'd have given anything to know what he was thinking.

"I don't mind buttoning it up," I told him.

"How did you know that was what I was thinking?"

My head jerked up. "What?"

"I was thinking that I could button the shirt on my own."

"You probably thought you were thinking it but said it out loud."

He nodded, but a crinkle appeared between his brows. Turning, I blew out a silent breath and made my way a few steps away from him.

The first time I read the man's mind, and it's about buttoning his shirt.

When I turned back to face him, Lucas was staring at me. "What?" I asked with a nervous laugh.

He shook his head. "Nothing. What brings you here?"

I chewed nervously on my lower lip as I looked at the basket, then at Lucas. "Well, you're probably going to think I'm crazy." I started to laugh, and that caused him to smile.

Before I could say anything else, his cell phone rang. "Hey, Mom. What? No, no, it's okay. I'll call Greg and see if he can come and pick me up and take me home."

For reasons unknown to me, I blurted out, "I can take you home!"

Lucas looked over at me with a surprised but happy expression. "Are you sure?"

I nodded as I wiped my hands on my jeans. Why were they sweating? Why had I offered to take him home? And maybe the sponge bath idea was looking good after all.

Turning, I shook my head and internally chastised myself.

Stop it, Hollie! Stop it!

"Yes, I'll be fine. I already promised the doctor I would not go to the dig site and take a couple of days off. I have food. Please stop worrying."

I couldn't help but smile. It was sweet that Rose wanted to make sure Lucas would be okay.

"Yes, I will let you know when I'm home." His eyes met mine. "I'll tell her both of those things."

My brows rose.

Hitting End, he smiled. "My mother said be careful driving, and hello."

"When are they going to give you your walking papers?" I asked.

Lucas reached for some papers that were sitting on the bed table. "Already got them. I'm ready to go whenever you are. I do think they are going to want me to leave in a stupid wheelchair, though."

"Right," I said. "I'll go find a nurse."

Quickly slipping out of the room, I leaned against the door once it shut and closed my eyes.

"He has that effect on you, doesn't he?"

My eyes snapped open to see a nurse standing there with a wheelchair.

"What? Who?"

She motioned with her head toward Lucas's door. "Mr. Dayton. All the nurses are talking about how handsome he is. Something about his eyes. Poor guy—he doesn't have very good luck, though."

"Why do you say that?" I asked as I pushed off the door.

"He was taking a shower earlier and slipped. Nearly fell. Luckily, I was there, and he reached for me before he tumbled. I'm not even sure how it happened. He was standing still."

"Wow, that's crazy."

Moving out of her way, I watched as she walked into Lucas's room. I followed, then came to a stop when I saw him looking in the basket I brought.

"Okay, Mr. Dayton, your chariot awaits."

Lucas looked at the nurse and gave her a polite smile, but when his eyes met mine, it widened. "What's this?"

I swallowed the lump in my throat and reached for the basket. Hopefully, he hadn't seen my written notes.

"Nothing," I softly said as I stepped out of the way of the nurse.

"Are you his ride?"

I wish.

"Yes," I said, pushing the instant dirty image out of my mind. "Yes. I'm here to give him a ride. I mean, take him home. In my car. I'm going to take him for a ride in my car to his house. That's all. That kind of ride."

They both looked at me. The nurse with a confused expression, and Lucas with his dimpled smile that made my insides quiver.

First thing I was going to ask Sarah about was whether there was a spell to make people forget things because the way Lucas was smiling at me said he wasn't going to let that Freudian slip go.

"If you don't mind heading down and getting your car, you can pull up at the main entrance, and we'll meet you there."

I smiled. "Of course. Right away. Here I go."

She stood there and stared at me like I had two heads.

Deciding it was best to just leave, I rushed out the door and to the elevators. Once I got outside, my phone rang, and I saw it was Kristin.

"Hello."

"Hey, what are you doing?"

I exhaled. "I'm about to take Lucas home."

"Wait, what? Oh, my gosh, did the spell work?"

"No. I mean, yes, but not the way we wanted. He's had a string of bad luck and got hit by a car and bruised his ribs. His mom wasn't able to do it, and I was there, so he asked me."

"Okay, wow. That was a lot to process. So, that is why you were at the hospital?"

With a quick look around, I lowered my voice some as I walked to my car. "Okay, listen to me carefully."

"I'm listening? Oh, this is going to be juicy. I can tell by the sound of your voice."

I rolled my eyes. "The spell worked, but it didn't work because apparently, we used the wrong spell, and it mixed with my true feelings for Lucas. So, it put a bad spell on him instead of, like, ripping him to pieces or crushing his bones—that kind of spell. And let me tell you, he has had a string of bad luck, all because of the stupid spell we did. Now, according to Lucy, I have to break the spell with another spell. So, I either give him a sponge bath with this special soap, or I talk him into letting me do another spell with him."

Pressing the unlock button on my key, I heard it beep.

"Kristin? Are you still there?"

"How much have you had to drink, honey?"

Sighing in frustration, I slipped into the car and started it. "I'm not drunk, Kristin. I think…I think…I think I'm really a witch?"

More silence.

"Do you know how many times you said spell?" Kristin asked. "I counted at least six, I think. What time do I need to come over with the whiskey?"

"I'm being serious! And I found out my mother practices the craft."

She gasped. "I knew it! I knew I walked in on your mother one time saying a spell when she was making pancakes!"

I decided to let that go and not even ask. "She hid it from me because apparently, I have some weird, freakish power or gift or whatever where I can feel things or see things before they happen. I don't know. All I know is I knew Lucas was hurt. I felt it."

"You felt it?"

"Yes! I have to go. I'm pulling up, and the nurse is making googly eyes at Lucas."

"Okay, this five-minute conversation had so much in it. I need to process all of this."

"Call you later! Love you! Bye!" I said as I hung up and tossed my purse into the back seat before getting out and rushing around to help the nurse help Lucas in.

"Honestly, I can get into the car," Lucas said as the nurse attempted to put her arm around him.

"He said he can get in," I snapped when she wouldn't get the hell out of the way.

Smiling, she handed me the discharge papers. "Please call his doctor if he has any problems."

I took the papers out of her hand and smiled. "Will do. Thank you!"

Lucas hit his head on the door and cursed as I closed my eyes and prayed I wouldn't get into a wreck on the way home.

Reaching into the car, I grabbed the seatbelt, pulled it across Lucas, and snapped it into the holder. Then I made the mistake of turning my head. Our faces were inches apart. Lucas's eyes fell to my mouth, and I licked my lips on impulse before I went to get out of the car and hit my own head on the doorframe.

"Ouch!" I cried out.

"Are you okay?" Lucas asked, a slight hint of laughter in his voice.

I rubbed my head and smirked. "I'm fine. Hands in."

After shutting the door, I walked around the back of the car and took in a few deep breaths. I would drug him with some painkillers, and he'd never remember it. Yes! That was the plan.

Slipping into the car, I smiled with my newfound courage. "Ready?"

He smiled back. "Ready."

My hands twisted together as I paced back and forth in Lucas's kitchen. That courage I found thirty minutes ago went right out the door when he informed me that he only needed a few Tylenol for the pain.

Now I was in his kitchen, supposedly to get water for the Tylenol while what I was really doing was freaking the hell out.

"Hey, what's going on?"

I stopped and turned to face Lucas.

Ugh. Why did he look extra handsome today?

When I didn't answer, he drew his brows down in concern. "Hollie, what is going on with you?"

Taking in a deep breath, I decided the best way to handle the problem was to just be honest.

Here goes nothing.

"Lucas, we have to talk."

"Okay, about what?"

I exhaled. "Let's get you that medicine and go sit in the living room where you'll be comfortable."

He agreed. After he took the Tylenol, we made our way back into the living room. Lucas carefully sat in the recliner, and I waited for him to get comfortable.

"You know, I don't need you to stay here, Hollie. I can manage on my own. It's just a couple of bruised ribs. I've got plenty of work I can do from home."

Smiling, I nodded. "I know you don't need me here. It's not that. I have a confession to make."

He raised his brows, and there was something in his eyes that almost looked...hopeful. I'd have to reflect on that later. Right now, I needed to sound like a crazy person and hope that he didn't throw me out of his house.

"Lucas, you know my sister, Sarah, and my Aunt Lucy."

Nodding, he said, "Of course, I do."

"And you also know they practice witchcraft. Not the bad kind that's fictional, but they're very in touch with nature and intuition. Very focused on heavenly bodies like the moon and stars."

The corner of his mouth tilted. "Yes, I'm aware of that. We have a number of people in Salem who practice witchcraft."

"Well, for years, my aunt has told stories about how the gift of witchcraft has been passed down from generation to generation."

"Even one of the women who was put to death in the Salem witch trials was an ancestor of your mom's, right?"

I nodded and started to twist my hands together. "Yes, there has always been a girl in our family with the name Sarah. It's a long story, but anyway, when I was little, I truly believed the stories Lucy would tell us. Then one day, it all kind of changed for reasons I wasn't really ready to admit to until the last day or so."

"Okay," he said in a concerned voice. "Is this going somewhere, Hollie?"

"Yes," I said as I placed my hands flat on my jeans. "I'm just going to say it. A couple nights ago, I got drunk with Kristin, and she talked me into putting a spell on you."

Lucas jerked his head back and gave me a stunned look. "A spell? You put a spell on me?"

"Yes! And why is that song now playing in my head?" I said with a nervous laugh. "You know, 'I put a spell on you, because you're mine...' Er...um...anyway, yes, I cast a spell on you. It was all in fun, though, because you see, I didn't think I was a witch at the time, or I was in really deep denial. And we used Halloween decorations, for goodness's sake."

"Okay."

"Anyway, the next morning, Sarah showed up claiming to have felt me use magick, and I, of course, laughed and brushed it off. Then she found out we—I mean, I—put a spell on you. It turns out, the spell I thought I was putting on you was not the spell I used, and because of some, um, *complications*, the spell went south."

"It went south?" he asked.

"Yeah, I mean, it is all jacked up. So, the spell I thought I was putting on you—all for fun, remember?—isn't actually the spell I put on you, and here's the best part!" I said with a nervous laugh.

"I can't wait to hear it," he deadpanned.

"It worked! Ha! Not in the way I wanted it to, but it worked. And that's why you're having all the bad luck."

Lucas stared at me for the longest time before he asked, "You think you really put a spell on me, and that's why I've had the string of bad luck?"

"Yes. It started the day after I put the spell on you. The nurse told me you almost slipped in the shower today, and you were standing still."

"That was just because the floor was slippery, Hollie. And the car accident was because some jackass was speeding through the parking lot."

"And the cut to your hand? The coffee? The stubbed toe?" I paused. "Wait, why were you in the shower? You were only in the hospital for a few hours."

"The IV bag they had burst and got all over me."

"What? How does an IV bag burst? Oh...right. Bad luck!" I stated.

He laughed, then quickly stopped. "You can't be serious right now."

"I'm dead serious, Lucas! And we need to do another spell to remove the bad spell."

Closing his eyes, I couldn't tell if he was struggling to keep from laughing or about to run away from me in total fear. When he opened his eyes, I sucked in a breath. It looked like fire danced in his eyes.

"If you didn't mean to put a bad spell on me, what were you trying to do?"

I swallowed hard. "Nothing."

"Nothing?" he asked, the corners of his mouth twitching with a hidden smile. "It had to be something, Hollie. Tell me what the spell was."

"It doesn't matter, Lucas," I said as I stood. "What matters is that we do this spell. It's either that or you take a bath and use this special soap."

"Is that what was in the basket you brought with you?" he asked.

"Yes, and some things for the reversal spell."

Lucas slowly moved to get out of the chair. "Hollie, are you feeling okay?"

"Lucas, I'm being serious! Why are you not taking this seriously?"

He went to stand, but something happened, and he started to lose his balance and was about to fall when I rushed over to help him steady himself.

"See? You were about to fall!"

"I lost my balance, for fuck's sake, Hollie."

Moving out of my hold, he turned and walked over to his bar cart. He took a whiskey glass and put it on the cart and went to open a bottle of whiskey. I watched as he poured a healthy glass, then downed it. He set the glass down and then turned to face me.

"Do you want a glass?"

I shook my head. I needed to keep a clear mind. I couldn't do that if I got drunk again, and that would only take a few glasses of whiskey.

"It's just a simple little spell, and it won't take more than five, ten minutes at the max."

He studied me for a moment, then smirked. "What if I want to take a bath with your magick soap?"

I frantically shook my head. "No, we can't do that one."

"Why not? Seems easy enough."

I worked my lips together in a nervous manner before I said, "I have to be the one to bathe you with the soap since I cast the spell."

Something moved over Lucas's face, but it was gone before I could read it.

Finally, he broke the weird spell we were both under. "Hollie, I'm tired, and I think I want to just lay down for a bit."

He started to move toward the sofa, and I saw what was about to happen before it happened. I didn't move in time, and Lucas tripped over a throw carpet. He started to fall forward and was trying to regain his balance when he hit the lamp on the side table next to the sofa. It teetered and he reached for it, causing him to further lose his balance. The lamp fell, breaking into pieces on the floor. Lucas turned around, yelled out in pain, then fell and hit his head on the coffee table.

"Oh, my God!" I screamed out as I rushed over to him. He was on the floor moaning, and when I tried to move him, he yelled out, "Stop! Wait. I need a minute. Can't. Breathe."

"Your ribs! Oh, my gosh! Lucas, you hit your face!"

He slowly rolled over, and my hand came up to my mouth as I gasped. He had hit his face, and his eye was already starting to turn black and blue. How was it happening so fast?

"I need to call your dad!" I said as I jumped up and ran to my purse to get my phone.

"Hollie, wait. Wait!" His voice sounded strangled. "It's okay, I barely hit the table. It's just my ribs. Can you help me up?"

I took a few steps away from him and shook my head. "What if I hurt you more?"

He looked at me, and I wanted to sink to my knees and beg him for forgiveness. All of this had been my fault. I hated myself in that moment. Hated that I was the reason he was in pain.

"Hollie, please just help me up and back over to the chair. Then can you clean up the broken lamp?"

"Yes! Of course," I said as I rushed over and carefully helped him stand. He put most of his weight on me as we both struggled to get him to the chair, where he carefully sat down, then leaned back into the chair and let out a sigh of relief.

I chewed on my lip as I watched him steady his heavy breathing. When he opened his eyes and looked at me, I gave him a weak smile.

"See? Bad luck."

He narrowed one eye at me, and for a moment I was sure he was about to lunge for my neck. My hand went to my neck, where I rubbed against the sudden tightness in there.

"I'll just clean up this mess. You rest. Here, let me get you another whiskey."

Slowly letting out a breath, Lucas dropped his head back and closed his eyes. I quickly poured him a drink and cleaned up the broken lamp.

Once everything was cleaned up, I sat down on the coffee table, only to see Lucas was asleep. I took the opportunity to look around his condo. This was the first time I had ever been in it, and I couldn't help but smile. It was located in a large federal mansion and was in the McIntire Historic District, which happened to be a pretty sought-after area of Salem. There were period details all throughout the house, at least based on what areas of the house I'd seen so far. Tall ceilings, original moldings, and stunning built-ins. Not to mention, he had beautiful, large windows that let in so much natural light. It was much nicer than my apartment. I liked my kitchen more; it was bigger. I loved to cook, so having a huge kitchen was a must.

The walls were painted a light gray with the trim painted white. It didn't have a bachelor vibe to it, so I couldn't help but wonder if someone had helped him decorate it.

I frowned. Maybe Wendy had. Ugh, the thought made me want to throw up.

"I can only imagine what you're thinking with that frown on your face."

My eyes jerked back to where he was sitting in the recliner. "I wasn't thinking anything. Just looking around the room. It's a very nice place you have here."

He smiled. "I think we need to get back to the ridiculous notion that you think you put a spell on me."

"Lucas, isn't it obvious? Have you ever had such bad like this before?"

He thought for a moment. "No. But I also don't think you're a witch and the cause of it. It's just a string of bad luck."

I could do this two ways: keep arguing my point or see if he would just go along with the spell. I decided to see if he would simply humor me.

"Fine, don't believe I'm a witch, but will you at least let me do the spell to reverse the bad luck? Please, Lucas."

Something in his eyes changed. Maybe it was witch's intuition, but I knew he was about to agree to let me do it.

Chapter Seven

Lucas

The moment she looked at me with those big blue eyes of hers, I knew I was going to let her do the stupid spell. For some reason, Hollie felt responsible for my...misfortunes the last few days, and if it meant she would spend more time with me, then I'd let her do it. Hell, at this point, I'd probably let her do anything she wanted, especially if she said my name like she just had.

"Fine, you can do the spell."

She jumped up, and I nearly lost my breath at the smile on her face. Shit, she was so beautiful.

"Great. You stay here, and I'll get it all ready. Don't move!"

I let out a grunt. "I'm not going anywhere."

My phone was sitting on the table next to me, so I picked it up and sent off a text to Manny to see how the dig was going. With winter approaching, we really needed to get as much work done as we could. Not to mention, the city wanted to build a park there and was on its own timeline.

Me: How are things going?

Manny: Good. Found some more artifacts. Don't worry, we're cataloging them and taking great care with each one. How are you feeling?

Me: Just a bit sore. I plan on being there tomorrow if I can get a good night's sleep and it doesn't feel like someone is stabbing me in my ribs.

Manny: LOL. Don't worry, Lucas. We've got this. I won't let you down.

Smiling, I looked into the dining room, to see Hollie busy with whatever the hell she was doing.

Me: I know you won't. Thanks, Manny. See you soon.

Taking another look to see Hollie still busy, I sent Shawn a text.

Me: Hollie seems to think she's the reason for my bout of bad luck.

It didn't take Shawn long to reply. My phone beeped less than a minute later.

Shawn: Why in the world would she think that?

Me: Ready for this?

Shawn: I'm not sure, but hit me.

Me: She said she put a spell on me.

My phone rang.

"Hey."

"Did I read that right? Hollie Craft thinks she put a spell on you? Did she hit her head or something?" asked Shawn.

I chuckled, then stopped when the pain shot through my side. "I'm not sure about that."

"I know her sister and aunt are into that, but where did she come up with that?"

"I can't say."

There was a moment of silence. "Dude, is she there with you now? Are you home?"

"I'm home. My mother wasn't able to help with that, so Hollie gave me a ride home."

"Hollie brought you home? How in the hell did that happen?"

"I can't comment on that right now, but I can get back to you on it."

"When did you get home?"

I glanced at the time on my phone. "Maybe an hour or less."

"And she's still there?"

"Yeah."

"Text me. I'm hanging up."

Before I could say anything, Shawn hung up, so I acted as if I was still speaking to someone. "Sounds good, keep me up to date with the progress. Thanks."

I hit End and noticed Hollie wasn't in the dining room, so I quickly sent off a text to Shawn.

Me: The short of it. She thinks she is a witch, got drunk the other night, and put a spell on me but says it was the wrong one, and it somehow put a jinx on me.

I watched as the three dots bounced.

Shawn: What was the spell supposed to be?

Me: I haven't figured it out yet.

Shawn: LOL. Good luck with all that.

Me: Thanks. Witching hour is about to begin. Later.

"Are you ready?"

Glancing up, I flashed her a smile. "I'll only do this if you tell me what spell you meant to put on me."

Her face went from ghost-white to bright-red. "Don't ask me to do that, Lucas. Please."

Damn it. What was it about the way she said please that made me want to give in to her?

I slowly stood. "I'll let it go for now, but I'm not going to drop this."

Her shoulders relaxed, and she let out a small sigh of relief.

"Okay, let's head into the dining room. I had to make this into an altar."

"An altar?" I asked as we made our way into the dining room. There was a candle in the middle of the table, a couple of bags that were filled with something, and a note she had written.

"Do you need help sitting down?"

I shook my head and sat in the chair. I wasn't about to tell her it was uncomfortable as hell. I was too curious to see how this all would play out.

"Okay. Now, I need you to take this seriously. Will you promise me, you will?"

Nodding, I crossed my heart.

Hollie sat down and drew in a deep breath. I could see her hands were shaking, yet she was super focused.

"We have to put a protective circle of salt around the candle."

"Like *Hocus Pocus*," I said, trying to sound serious.

She shot me a dirty look, and I held my hands up. "Sorry. Serious."

I watched her as she carefully put a circle of salt around the candle.

Glancing at her notes, she looked at me. "We both need to take a deep breath. Or wait, maybe I'm supposed to take it. No, you are! Shit. I think you were supposed to pour the salt. Fuck!"

I watched as she quickly cleaned up the salt, put it in the bag, then handed it to me. When she held it out, she was still shaking.

"You really believe this, don't you?" I asked.

She blinked a few times, chewed on her lip, then answered, "I do."

"Okay," I softly said as I took the bag and stood. I poured a circle around the candle, then sat back down.

"Deep breath," she whispered.

I took about as deep of a breath as my bruised ribs would let me.

"Now, say this after me: Bad luck, I command you to leave me right now."

I stared at her for a moment, and when she looked at me with pleading eyes, I repeated her words.

"Um, bad luck, I command you to leave me right now."

She smiled and my heart felt like it skipped a beat.

Handing me matches, she told me to light the candle.

"Now, take a moment to visualize how bad luck has been affecting you the last couple of days."

I was about to argue, but I saw the earnest expression on her face and in her eyes. I closed my eyes and pictured everything that had happened. It wasn't until I actually thought about it that I realized a lot of crazy shit had happened to me. Maybe...no way.

After a minute of reflection, Hollie spoke. "Now, repeat after me: All adversity now dissolves."

I repeated her words.

"Now, I need you to close your eyes again and picture an empty canvas."

"An empty canvas?"

She nodded. "Yes, it's like a do-over."

I sighed and did what she asked.

"Fill it with whatever you want to attract."

One eye opened and I looked at her. "What I want to attract?"

"Yes, like good fortune, a successful dig, things that would make you happy and fulfill your world."

A kiss from the woman sitting across from me, for starters.

Yeah, I couldn't say that out loud, so I nodded.

"Take your time," she whispered.

It didn't take long for my thoughts to conjure up images of Hollie. Her in my arms. Her mouth on mine. Her hands in my hair. The way she might whisper my name as I made love to her. I quickly got lost in the lustful daydreams.

When I realized my cock was getting as hard as a rock, I opened my eyes to find her staring at me. Her upper teeth were dug into her lower lip, and I reached over to pull it out. Her breath hitched and I swore something cracked in the air between us.

"You um...um... You have to sprinkle the cinnamon over the circle of salt."

She produced another bag filled with what I was guessing was cinnamon. I took it and when our fingers brushed against each other, we paused. Had she felt the rush of energy that passed between us? No, it wasn't energy, it was desire.

"Sprinkle the cinnamon?" I asked.

Nodding, she said, "Over the salt."

I made little piles of cinnamon all around the salt, then handed her back the bag.

"Now what?"

She blinked a few times. "Say after me: Only good luck and positive energy flows to me now."

With a half-smile, I said, "Only good luck and positive energy flows to me now."

She let out a relieved breath that was a half-laugh. "Good. Now, visualize how the candle is absorbing the protective energy of the salt. The cinnamon adds a burst of good luck. Now, close your eyes and meditate for a few minutes as you replace the bad with good."

We stared at one another for the longest time before I finally closed my eyes. Thoughts of Hollie once again filled my mind. The look on her face when she rushed into the hospital. How dark her eyes turned when she saw me without my shirt on. The way she smiled at me, and it touched her eyes.

When she spoke, she pulled me out of my thoughts.

"The candle needs to burn down completely. Once it's burned all the way down, you'll need to bury it in soil and say thank you."

I reached for her hand and held it, trying like hell to ignore the fire that raced through my body at the feel of her hand in mine. "Do you feel better now?"

She nodded. "Do you?"

"If I'm being honest, I feel the same."

A bubble of laughter slipped free from her lips, and I found that I loved that sound a whole lot.

"It's dangerous to leave a candle going—you know that."

"Well...," she replied as she looked at the candle. "As long as you're home and can watch it, it should be okay."

I nodded. "What if I fall asleep? Who will watch it for me?"

Her tongue came out and darted across her lips. "I suppose, I mean, I could stay and watch for you. If you wanted."

My eyes drifted down to her mouth, and it took every ounce of strength I had to keep from pulling her to me and kissing the hell out of her.

"I want that."

"You do?" she softly asked.

"Yes."

Her chest rose and fell, and for a moment, I thought for sure she was going to lean over and kiss me. She suddenly stood, causing the chair to scrape across the wood floor. "Are you hungry? I could make you something to eat?"

Out of the corner of my eye, I saw the note she had been reading from. There was something else written on it, and I wanted to know what it said.

"You don't have to make me anything, Hollie."

"Yes, I do. I mean, I'm hungry too."

"Okay," I said with a smile. "I'm not sure what all I have."

"I'll find something. Do you need help getting back to the living room?"

"No, I'm going to sit here and...meditate for a bit."

A wide smile spread over her face. "Wonderful! I won't be long."

Once she was in the kitchen, I reached for the paper, ignoring the sharp pain in my side.

My eyes went wide as I read her notes about the soap. When Hollie walked back in, she froze.

"What are you doing?"

Looking up at her, I flashed her a wicked smile. "Had I known that was an option, I'd have picked the bath."

Hollie placed the plate on the table that contained a sandwich, chips, and some fruit. She sat down, put her plate down, and began to eat.

"You have nothing to say to that?"

Shrugging, she replied, "I'm sure something smartass will come out of your mouth if I do."

I narrowed my eyes at her. "What do you mean?"

She looked up and our eyes met. "I'm not the type of woman you typically go for, Lucas. Besides, we don't like each other in that way."

"We don't?" I asked.

Her throat bobbed as she worked to swallow.

"Seems to me you might like me a bit since you've gone to all this trouble and offered to stay until the candle burned out," I said.

Clearing her throat, she said, "I'm just trying to make up for a mistake."

We ate in silence for a few minutes before I broke it. "Are you going to tell me what spell you thought you were putting on me?"

"No."

"That's not fair, you know. You show up with these crazy ideas, and I go along with them, and you won't even tell me what you were trying to do to me?"

"It's not like that, Lucas. I had been drinking, and I let Kristin talk me into it."

"And now you believe you're a witch?"

She gave me a one-shoulder shrug. "I don't know what to believe, but it's the only reason I can think of for why you had all the bad luck."

"Hollie, it was just a few days of bad luck. That's it."

"And earlier? The broken lamp? Your black eye?"

I reached up, touched under my eye, and winced. It hurt like a son of a bitch.

"You can't explain it, but I can. Listen, I know it sounds crazy, Lucas. A couple days ago, if someone would have come to me with all of this, I would have said the same thing. But something changed. I don't know how to explain it."

"You truly think you're a witch?"

"Not in the way you think. Being a witch isn't about broomsticks and pointed hats and black cats. It's a belief. It's being in touch with nature."

"And the moon and stars?"

She rolled her eyes.

"I'm sorry," I said as I reached for her hand once again. She didn't pull it away, and that made my heart beat a little stronger in my chest.

"You said you felt it when I was hurt. What did you mean?"

She shook her head. "I don't know how to describe it. Something told me you'd been hurt. Like an intuition. A feeling rather than a conscious reasoning. I just knew."

"Like when you answered me before I even asked the question, and don't say I asked it out loud because I know I didn't."

Exhaling, she replied, "Yes. My aunt told me that when I was younger, I came running into the house upset because my brother had fallen and gotten hurt. When my parents rushed outside, they saw him fall and get hurt. I had somehow seen it or knew that it was about to happen before it did. It was then that my mother decided she would not practice the craft in front of me."

Frowning, I asked, "Your mom practices witchcraft too?"

"Yes. Well, she did. I think she might still, but she's put on a show of not believing in it. Lucy said she was afraid because I possessed this gift or power or whatever you want to call it, and I was so young. She thought if I didn't believe in the craft, then it wouldn't happen again. She thought it was too powerful for someone so young."

"I remember, in school, you would answer the teacher sometimes before she would even ask a question."

She nodded. "I was teased a lot, so I'm sure that is another reason I pushed it out of my head."

Hollie suddenly stood, took both plates, and then headed for the kitchen.

I got up and followed her. Standing in the doorway, I watched her as she rinsed off the plates and put them in the dishwasher. She turned to face me.

"Tell me the spell, Hollie."

She slowly shook her head. "I can't."

I moved further into the kitchen, and she started to back away from me. "Why won't you tell me?"

Hollie started to wring her hands in what I had quickly realized was a nervous manner. I stopped only inches away from her. Our eyes locked onto each other's, and I leaned down closer to her.

"Tell me."

"Please, Lucas. Don't ask me to tell you," she said in a husky voice that seemed to travel straight to my dick. Fuck, if I didn't want this girl.

Lifting my hand, I reached up and took one of the curls that hung down just below her shoulders. Her light brown hair was naturally curly, and she usually wore it up, but today, it was down. The long-sleeve, blue T-shirt she had on made her eyes pop even more than usual. They reminded me of deep, blue pockets of the ocean. So blue, they took your breath away.

"Hollie," I whispered as I moved my mouth to the side of her ear. Her entire body shivered, and I loved that she reacted to me like that. "Tell me what the spell was for."

She inhaled and I was almost sure she was going to say it. Then her hands came up, and she pressed them to my chest, causing a rush of energy to move from her body to mine. I moved my head and placed a soft kiss on her neck.

Gently pushing me away, Hollie ducked under my arm. "What are you doing?"

I turned to face her. "What do you mean?"

"You kissed me."

"Did I?"

She looked confused as her hand came up and touched the spot on her neck where I had placed a kiss.

"Why won't you tell me the spell, Hollie?"

"I'm afraid to."

I frowned. "Why?"

She licked her lips and tangled her hands together. "I'm afraid you won't feel the same way."

My knees nearly buckled. I needed to know what the hell that spell was for.

"Please tell me."

She was about to say something when another voice filled the room.

"What's going on?"

Hollie spun around so fast, she nearly lost her balance. Then she gasped when she saw Wendy standing there.

"How did you get in?" I asked, my voice laced with both anger and confusion.

Wendy pulled her heated gaze off Hollie and forced a smile. "I knocked. You didn't answer so I tried the door, and it was unlocked. Greg said you came home. I've called your cell a number of times, and you didn't answer. I was worried so I came over. Why is she here?"

"She?" Hollie asked, her voice dripping with anger. "She has a name, Wendy."

With a dramatic roll of her eyes, Wendy clarified, "Why are you here, Hollie?"

Then she looked at me once again and slapped her hand over her mouth.

"What happened?" she asked as she rushed over to me. "You have a black eye!"

It was then I noticed the bumps on her face. "What happened to your face and neck?"

Wendy took a few steps back and cleared her throat. "I got this weird rash earlier today. Right after I left the hospital. I think it was from stress over worrying about you."

My gaze immediately went to Hollie. Her words from earlier came back. "*I hope she gets a rash all over her body.*"

Then I remembered what she had said to me a few days ago when I asked about her inner witch.

"*When you get the body rash that won't stop itching, then you'll know I've found her.*"

All she did was smile and shrug when our gazes met.

"Looks like it hurts," Hollie stated as she leaned against the door jam.

Ignoring Hollie, Wendy focused on my face. "Did she do this?"

"What?" Hollie and I both asked at the same time.

"I'm sorry, are you accusing me of not only attempting to hit the man with my car, but now you also think I'm physically hitting him?"

Wendy faced Hollie. "I wouldn't put it past you! There is something off with you, Hollie Craft. I've always known it. You've always been weird and different with your...your..."

Suddenly, Hollie got a Cheshire cat smile on her face. "Why, are you afraid to say it? You weren't when we were younger, and you used to chant it while throwing rocks at me."

"Wait, what?" I asked.

Wendy looked panicked. "I don't know what you mean."

Hollie moved closer to Wendy. "I'm a witch so I would probably stop accusing me of trying to hurt Lucas before I get mad."

It took everything I had not to start laughing. The look on Wendy's face was priceless.

"You're crazy." She looked back at me. "She's crazy, Lucas. Why do you have her in your house?"

I half-shrugged. "She wanted to do a spell, so we did one together." I pointed to the dining room, and Wendy looked past Hollie, then gasped.

"You're practicing dark magick?"

Hollie laughed. "Oh, for the love, Wendy. Stop with that nonsense. You sound like someone from the Salem witch trials."

Wendy spun around and glared at Hollie. "If you think you can put one of your hocus pocus spells on Lucas to make him like you, then you are crazier than I thought you were."

For a brief moment, the look on Hollie's face faltered. If I hadn't been watching her so closely, I would have missed it.

"He could *never* want someone like you," Wendy hissed.

"That's enough, Wendy," I said as I started toward her. "You have no right coming into my home and treating a friend of mine like that."

Wendy let out a bark of laughter. "Since when has she become a friend of yours? You've even said in the past she gets under your skin. That she is the last person on earth you'd ever want to be friends with."

I flinched. I had said those words—though not all of them—a long time ago when I was angry with Hollie for winning something we had both gone out for.

A low growl of anger came from the back of my throat. "It's time for you to leave, Wendy."

"It's fine, I'll go."

At Hollie's words, I turned around to look at her. "What?"

She forced a smile, but I could see the hurt in her eyes. "I'll leave. Just remember not to blow out the candle until it burns out."

"No, Hollie, wait."

With the pain in my side, I wasn't able to keep up with how fast she moved past me. She grabbed her purse, the basket, and her coat.

"Hollie, will you just wait a second! Stop, goddamn it!" I shouted as she opened the front door. Ignoring me, she rushed out and slammed the door behind her.

"Fuck!" I said as I scrubbed my hand down my face, flinching again at the pain under my eye and on my side.

"Good riddance. She's an awful person."

Anger filled my body with such force, I wanted to punch something. "Get out, Wendy."

"I'm sorry?" she asked as she walked up and put her hand on my arm. "Lucas, you don't... You don't like her, do you?"

I stepped away and faced her. "Get out of my house now, Wendy. And don't ever walk in like you have a right to. If I don't answer the door, that means I don't want to see you."

Her eyes went wide while her mouth dropped open.

When she didn't move, I walked to the door, opened it, and motioned for her to leave.

"You're going to regret this, Lucas."

"Somehow, I seriously doubt that."

Wendy huffed and marched out the front door. This time, it was me who slammed it shut.

I walked straight to my phone and opened my text messages. I found Kristin in my contacts.

Me: Hey, it's Lucas. I was wondering if we might be able to meet for breakfast tomorrow. There's something I need to talk to you about.

Kristin: Something or someone?

Christ, were they all witches?

Me: Hollie.

Again, I watched the little bubbles move across my screen.

Kristin: Meet you at Ugly Mug Diner, 8:30 sharp.

Me: See you then.

My body suddenly ached from head to toe. I walked into the dining room, grabbed the soap Hollie had left behind, and headed to my bathroom. A hot bath would do wonders for me.

Chapter Eight

Lucas

I saw Kristin the moment I stepped into the Ugly Mug Diner. Her dark-blonde hair was pulled back into a ponytail. Her face was planted in a book as she twirled a spoon in her coffee.

"Thanks for meeting me," I said as I slid into the chair across from her, ignoring the pain.

The book came down, and she shot me a dirty look. "I should really kick your ass."

I paused and raised a single brow. "May I ask why?"

"My very best friend was so upset last night, I couldn't even understand her when she was trying to talk. I still don't know why, but I know it has something to do with you."

Sighing, I leaned back in the chair. "A misunderstanding, that's all."

Kristin also sat back in her seat and folded her arms, giving me a look that said she didn't believe me at all.

"It was a...crazy afternoon, Kristin. Hollie told me everything, about the spells, the bad-luck curse. Then Wendy stopped by and spewed out some bullshit I said about Hollie when we were in high school, not all of which was true. Hollie got pissed and stormed out, and now she won't take my calls."

Kristin's mouth dropped open as she leaned forward and whispered, "She told you about the spells? Both spells?"

I nodded, even though I knew it was wrong to mislead her.

"She also told me she now thinks she is a witch."

Kristin laughed. "I've always believed she had some sort of magickal powers. I swear, she can sometimes hear your thoughts before you even voice them."

I nodded. "She answered a question I hadn't even asked yet."

Pointing at me, Kristin nodded. "Yes! It's creepy-weird. She does it to me all the time."

The waitress came up and asked for my drink order. After ordering a cup of coffee and the deluxe egg sandwich, I focused back on Kristin. She was staring at me with a look I couldn't read.

"What is it?"

She slowly shook her head. "I can't believe she would tell you about the first spell. I mean, she's kept her feelings for you so locked up inside. I told her to tell you how she felt, but she was so afraid of rejection by you or of you not feeling the same way about her."

My heart nearly jumped out of my chest, but I forced myself to keep a neutral expression. I just hoped Kristin couldn't see how fast my pulse was beating in my neck 'cause it felt like my heart was going to pop out of my body.

"I think she was scared because of the few little accidents I had. She wanted to come clean."

Kristin chuckled. "Well, when we found out we did a sunder spell and not a notice-me spell, it didn't seem to matter at first. It was all just a joke, until, well, it wasn't."

"She didn't tell me, though, how the spell got mixed up."

Kristin frowned. "She didn't?"

"Well, bits and pieces, but Wendy interrupted us, and then Hollie got pissed, and now she won't answer my calls or texts, like I said."

Kristin smirked. "Sounds like her. All I know is, Lucy told her that because she has romantic feelings for you, by using the wrong spell, it kind of confused the spell. We thought we were putting a spell on you to notice her, you know, in a more romantic way. Turns out, it was to put you in sunder. But because of how she felt toward you, it made the spell turn into, like, a bad-luck spell instead of a hurt-you-really-bad spell. Well, needless to say, Hollie didn't believe Sarah at first until you were hit by that car."

My mind was in a tailspin. Hollie had romantic feelings for me? I wanted to ask Kristin a million questions. What kinds of feelings? How long had she had these feelings? Why in the hell did she act like she couldn't stand me all those years? Oh, wait...I had done the same damn thing.

"Lucas?"

Snapping my head up, I asked, "Sorry, what did you say?"

"Do you think the reversal spell worked?"

I blinked a few times. I'd stayed up damn near all night watching the fucking candle burn. Once it burned out, I was in my backyard this morning digging a hole to bury it in. Mrs. Dodger, my eighty-year-old neighbor, probably thought I was burying a body.

"I don't know. Nothing has happened to me at all this morning."

Kristin smiled. "Well, I know Hollie has tried to deny her gift, but I think her mind has changed."

I nodded. "Yeah, it sure seems like it."

"So, how did it make you feel knowing Hollie has liked you all these years? You didn't say anything hurtful to her when she told you, did you?"

Moving around in my seat, I rubbed at the back of my neck and looked around the restaurant, avoiding eye contact with Kristin.

"You bastard. She didn't tell you about the first spell, did she?"

Finding the courage to look at Kristin, I shook my head. "No. She was about to, though. Then Wendy came in, and things went to shit."

Kristin's boot landed a good kick on my shin, and I jumped, then nearly screamed out in pain from my ribs.

"Fucking hell! Why did you do that? I have bruised ribs. What in the hell is wrong with all you women?"

"You lied to me, Lucas Dayton! You lying bastard!"

"I didn't really lie. I just... I just...didn't tell you the truth."

She folded her arms over her chest. "That's the same thing." Then her arms dropped, and a horrified expression crossed her face. "Lucas, you can't tell her I told you. She would be so mad at me and so embarrassed. Especially if you don't feel the same way about her."

"I won't say anything to her."

Kristin tilted her head and gave me a look that said she was waiting for me to say more.

"What?"

"You're not going to tell me how you feel about my best friend?"

"I'm almost afraid to tell you anything."

"As you should be. Now spill it, Dayton."

Drawing in a deep breath, I exhaled. "I've secretly liked Hollie since middle school."

Kristin gasped, slapped both hands over her mouth, and started to jump around in her seat. Nearly the entire restaurant was now watching us.

"Would you stop acting like a child, Kristin?"

After getting herself under control, Kristin leaned across the table. "All the years you two idiots have wasted. And you slept with Wendy Hoffman. Gross, Lucas! Gross!"

I rolled my eyes. "I haven't been with her in years."

"Are you going to tell her?"

"I don't know."

"What do you mean, you don't know?" she asked, looking as if she was readying her foot to kick me once again.

"I mean, I don't know how to tell her. Because if I say something now, she'll think it's because of that stupid spell."

Kristin shook her head so hard, I thought it might come off and roll right out the door of the restaurant. "She won't, Lucas. The spell was wrong. She never put that kind of spell on you, unless..."

Her voice trailed off as she frowned and looked deep in thought.

"Unless what?" I asked.

Glancing up at me, she answered, "Unless she did it again but with the right spell. I mean, you can't alter someone's heart. All she wanted was for you to notice her."

I let out a humorless laugh. "I've been noticing her for years."

A soft smile played across her face. "But she doesn't know that. You have to find a way to tell her that without her thinking it's because of some spell."

"I don't believe in spells, Kristin."

She blew out a long breath. "Yeah, but the problem is, Hollie does. And that's going to confuse her even more than she already was."

A feeling of dread washed over me, and I wasn't even sure why.

"Listen, is Hollie going to the Salem Witches' Halloween Ball next Sunday?" I asked.

The ball was an annual event held the night before Halloween. starting at sundown.

"Of course. We never miss it."

A small bubble of excitement started to brew up inside of me as an idea formed. "Great. Just make sure she's there. I'll handle the rest."

Kristin gave me a quizzical look, but thankfully, didn't ask any questions.

The waitress brought over our food and set it on the table. After asking us if we needed anything more, Kristin reached for her orange juice.

"Shall we toast?"

Reaching for my glass of water, I asked, "To what?"

A wide smile erupted on Kristin's face. "To the newest witch in Salem."

I clinked my glass with hers. "To the newest witch in Salem."

Chapter Nine

Hollie

Kristin held up a dress, if you could call it that, and smiled brightly. I stared at it before I busted out laughing.

"You want me to wear that?"

She looked at the orange dress that I was positive wouldn't even cover my ass and nodded.

"Yes. I have these black and orange thigh-high stockings, and your black high-heel boots will finish it off."

"Does she have a black witch's hat too?" Sarah asked as she walked into my room. I had invited her over earlier in the day to have lunch with our mom and Lucy. Needless to say, my mother was over the moon that she could finally come out of the broom closet.

The last week, I had done nothing but throw myself into work. I had everything ready for the three events I had for tomorrow, including Greg's engagement. Lucas has called me a number of times, and whenever I had to meet with him, I made sure someone else was there. Nathan had stepped in and helped me move a lot of stuff from my warehouse to Dayton's barn yesterday since Lucas's ribs were bruised.

Lucas hadn't known it, but I had checked in on him a few times at the dig site and had followed him home from work Friday night. Everything seemed to be fine—no more accidents. Kristin had mentioned she ran into him one morning, and he mentioned not having any bad luck. The reversal spell must have worked. Sarah, Mom, and Lucy had all assured me it had earlier today.

I'd spent the last week going over spells and different things with Sarah each night after we both finished working. I hated to admit it to anyone, let alone myself, but it all felt so right. It seemed to just click. We even went to my parents' house and went through my mother's massive outdoor garden and greenhouse. Mom admitted to me she was part of a coven of witches here in Salem that also included Sarah and Aunt Lucy. And they had been keeping one spot open... for me.

"What are you wearing?" I asked my sister.

"The same thing I wear every year," Sarah replied.

Kristin groaned. "Not the black dress and black cape. Sarah, it's 2022. Can you please dress it up a bit? Nothing says a modern witch can't look stylish."

Sarah laughed.

Kristin gasped. "Oh, my God. What if that's my calling? A stylist to the witches of Salem."

Pointing to the dress I now held in my hands, my sister replied, "It will be a cold day in hell before I wear something like that."

I couldn't help but laugh. "Okay, it is cute, I will say that."

A wide smile broke out over Kristin's face. "I'm telling you, you won't regret wearing it. You'll feel sexy. And all those bitches who used to make fun of you for being a witch will eat crow because you'll be the sexiest witch in Salem."

Turning to look into my full-length mirror, I exhaled. "Since a spell didn't get Lucas to look at me differently, maybe this dress will."

My eyes lifted to see Sarah and Kristin exchange a knowing look. Kristin had hinted a few times over the last week that Lucas seemed to be very upset by what Wendy had said. I knew he had because he had texted me a dozen or more times. He also assured that he had never said that I was the last person he would ever want to be friends with. Then he said something interesting—that Wendy was jealous of me. I wanted to dig deeper into that, but I was tired of giving her any of my attention.

"We could always try another spell," Sarah stated.

Turning, I looked at her as I chewed on my bottom lip. For a crazy few seconds, I almost agreed. "No," I said with a shake of my head. "That's not how I want it to be. If Lucas is interested in me, I want it to happen naturally. Not with any help."

"You said he kissed you in his kitchen on the neck," Kristin stated.

My hand went up to the spot.

"And that he almost kissed you on the lips until Wendy walked in. Well, we could do a simple love charm."

I looked at Kristin who had one brow raised. "Then you would never know if it was the spell or not."

"Maybe I should just forget about Lucas. Do you have a spell for that?" I asked my sister.

"I'm afraid not," she replied as she reached for my hand. "Just have fun tonight, Hollie."

Standing up straighter, I squared off my shoulders and put the little dress up against my body. "I think I will. And whatever happens, happens. I can't stay out late tonight, though, because I have three events to set up tomorrow, so it will be an early evening for me."

Sarah walked over and kissed me on the cheek, then pulled me in for a hug. "I'm so glad you're finally opening your mind to your gifts, Hollie."

I returned the gesture and hugged her in return. "I'm still not sure if it was all just a coincidence or a bit of hocus pocus."

Sarah winked. "Maybe a little of both. Gotta run and get ready. I'm picking up Mom, Dad, and Lucy. See you guys there!"

"See ya later," I called out, then turned back to Kristin.

"Will you let me do your hair?" she asked.

Laughing, I nodded.

Kristin jumped on the bed and clapped. "Let's get started."

Nearly two hours later, I stood in front of the same mirror and gaped at the transformation. The little witch's dress fell to the middle of my thighs. The thigh-high stockings came up a few inches above my knees, and the high-heel black boots really made the outfit look sexier than it should have. My hair was pulled up and piled on top of my head in endless curls. My makeup was light, how I liked it, but I was wearing bright-red lipstick that Kristin said was the one thing that pulled the entire outfit together.

Placing her chin on my shoulder, Kristin giggled. "You are going to turn some serious heads tonight in this outfit."

I felt my cheeks heat. There was only one man I wanted to get the attention of, and I wasn't even sure he would be there. Maybe I shouldn't have avoided him so hard this past week. I was just so confused and, if I was being honest, scared.

"Ready?" Kristin asked.

Turning, I looked at the black dress that hugged Kristin's curves. She wore bright-orange boots and a matching orange hat. She handed me a hat, and I shook my head. "No hat for me tonight."

"Okay, if you say so."

Forty minutes later, we were walking in the front doors of the Hawthorne Hotel, where the Salem Witches' Halloween Ball was taking place. For some reason, I was nervous, and my stomach felt jittery.

"What's wrong?" Kristin asked as we made our way toward the ballroom.

"I don't know. I feel like something is... Something is..."

"Something is what?"

"About to change but in a good way."

With a smirk, she wrapped her arm with mine. "I think you're right."

We walked into the room to find it packed as usual. The annual ball was a costume party and an event where people could speak and interact freely with those who practiced Witchcraft. There would be Tarot cards, folk magick, spells, crystals, astrology, ceremonial magick, and so much more. And food. There would be some amazing food as well as it just being a really fun time.

Walking farther into the room, I stopped to read the food menu.

Warm Brie Dip
Buffalo Cauliflower with a blue cheese dip
Chicken and Lemon Tacos
Veggie Egg Rolls
Cheese Boards
Fruit Boards
Mediterranean Station

"I say we hit up the Mediterranean Station. Those marinated olives and grilled veggies sound like heaven!" I said as my hand covered my growling stomach.

Kristin grabbed my hand, and we wound our way through the crowd, stopping to say hello to friends along the way.

"Hollie?"

The sound of my name caused me to stop. Turning, I saw Shawn, Lucas's best friend.

"Hi, Shawn."

He made no effort to hide the fact that his gaze was sweeping over my body. "You look amazing."

"Doesn't she, though?" Kristen agreed. "We're on our way to get some food. Toodles!"

Pulling me by the arm, Kristin practically dragged me away from Shawn.

"That was rude," I said as we walked up to the food table and each took a plate. I started to pile grilled veggies onto my plate as Kristin huffed.

"Please, he has the hots for you and wasn't even trying to hide the fact that he was eye-fucking you. If Lucas saw the way he was staring at you, he'd punch him."

"Kristin!" I cried out with a laugh.

"It's true."

Next to the grilled veggies, I set some marinated olives, along with some roasted bell peppers and marinated artichokes.

"We're never going to find a place to sit down and eat," I called out over the music playing.

"Follow me! We're sitting with some friends!" Kristin said as she made her way through the crowd. "Dark Horse" by Katy Perry started to play, and so many people went to the dance floor.

Kristin walked up to a table that had a few people sitting at it and motioned for me to sit down. I glanced around to see the other people at the table all worked with Lucas.

"Hey, guys! We've been waiting for you," Manny said as he stood and held out a chair for me. I sat as we all exchanged hellos, then I shot Kristin a questioning look. She simply smiled and shrugged.

Before I even had a chance to take a bite of food, I felt a shiver run down my back. Warm breath tickled my neck as Lucas spoke against my ear.

"So, you wanna play with magick?"

My eyes darted up to see no one at the table watching as Lucas mimicked the words of the song into my ear. I tilted my neck and felt goosebumps erupt over my skin at the heat of his breath hitting it.

"What kind of magick are you talking about?" I turned in my seat to look up at him. The air caught in my lungs as I took in Lucas. He wore a vintage, black tailcoat jacket and a black Victorian frock coat. It was topped off with a black top hat. He was also carrying a walking stick. My eyes moved over his body, and I had to remember how to speak.

"Who are you supposed to be?" I asked.

He looked surprised before the corner of his mouth rose into a sexy smirk. "Why, I would think a witch would recognize a warlock."

I raised a single brow. "A warlock?"

Extending his hand, he waggled his brows. "Dance with me?"

When I stood, he let his eyes roam my body, and I could see the lust in them. I couldn't even put into words how that made me feel. Happy. Nervous. Excited.

"You look beautiful, Hollie."

My cheeks flushed, and I was so thankful I hadn't had Sarah do a spell.

And as if I had summoned her up, my sister appeared. She was wearing an outfit almost like mine but a bit lower and not as short.

"Sarah, you let Kristin style you!"

She rolled her eyes. "I did. And no, I did not use a spell."

I blinked several times. She had read my mind.

Leaning in, she whispered, "You're not the only one with that particular gift."

When she sat down in my spot, she said, "I'm starving!"

Laughing, I focused back on Lucas. "I'd love to dance."

He placed my hand over his arm and led us to the dance floor. As we passed by the DJ, Lucas tipped his hat, then drew me into his arms as we waited for the next song to start.

The moment Frank Sinatra's "Witchcraft" started to play, I couldn't help but smile.

"You think I'm crazy, don't you?" I asked as I looked up into his soft, brown eyes that danced with amusement.

He spun me and pulled me closer to him. "At first, I thought you had lost your damn mind, Hollie."

"Fair enough."

"But, if you believe it, then I believe it too."

My heart started to beat harder in my chest. "Why?"

A sexy smile played across his face. "Because there's no nicer witch than you, and I happen to be head over heels for you, Hollie Craft. I'd follow you to the moon and back if you asked me to."

"What?" I whispered.

He placed his hand on the side of my face, leaned down, and rubbed his nose with mine. "I have been hot for you since middle school."

A bubble of laughter slipped free as I shook my head in disbelief. "I've been hiding my feelings for you as well."

Lucas shook his head. "And you say, you're a witch? You couldn't read my mind on that subject?"

"I guess not," I said with a smirk.

Lucas placed his mouth next to my ear. "I have a feeling this is going to be an interesting ride, but I wouldn't miss it for the world."

His mouth captured mine, and I instantly melted into his embrace. Lucas held me closer and moaned when I opened to him. Our tongues moved in a rhythmic dance, and everything and everyone disappeared.

When he slowly drew away and leaned his forehead to mine, I fought to pull air into my lungs. When I could finally speak, I asked, "Is this a dream?"

Lucas placed his finger on my chin and lifted my gaze to meet him. "I've been waiting a long time to kiss you, my little witch."

A burst of happiness exploded in my chest. "I swear, I didn't put another spell on you."

He threw his head back and laughed, then quickly stopped. The pain on his face reminded me that he had bruised ribs.

"Lucas! Your ribs."

"Are fine. Would you be upset if we left?"

"The only person who is going to be upset if I leave is Kristin. She had grand plans of showing me off in this little outfit."

A low growl came from the back of Lucas's throat. "I can't stand the way men are looking at you. I nearly punched my best friend in the face when he said you looked hot as hell."

"Hot as hell, huh?"

He grinned and I reached up to brush a kiss across his soft lips. "I'm ready to leave whenever you are."

That was all it seemed to take for Lucas. He grabbed my hand and started to guide us through the crowd of people. A few people attempted to stop and talk to him about the new dig, and he brushed them off with an excuse that he had to leave to take care of something important. No one seemed to question that he was pulling along a witch in his wake.

Once we were outside, Lucas stepped down and whistled for a carriage that was waiting down the street.

"Are you cold?" he asked as I rubbed my hands over my arms. I was regretting not wearing a coat. "We can take a taxi."

I shook my head. "They'll have a blanket."

The carriage stopped, and Lucas helped me up, then asked for the driver to take us as close to his home address as he could. As he lived right off Essex Street, it wouldn't be an issue.

Lucas climbed in next to me and placed the blanket over both of us before he wrapped his arm around me and drew me next to his body.

"Did something happen since I last saw you?" I asked.

"Yes, I realized I was tired of hiding my feelings for you, and I was going to do something about it."

"We've been stupid."

He nodded. "And stubborn."

"That too."

I leaned my head on his shoulder and chewed nervously on my lip before I said, "Lucas, I was being completely serious when I asked you to do the reversal spell."

"I know," he softly said as he kissed the top of my head.

"And you're okay with me exploring this?"

"You mean your belief that you're a witch? I know lots of people who believe in witchcraft, Hollie. I don't look at it as something bad. My mother has used a healer my entire life. And my father is a doctor."

"I think it goes a bit more than just your typical 'in tune with mother earth' and all of that. I hear people's thoughts. And the day of your accident. I felt it deep in my bones, and the ache in my heart was almost unbearable."

"So, what you're really saying is that you have a connection with me... One might even call it...love."

I moved my body some to look at him. My eyes searched his face, and I followed my heart. "Yes, one might."

His soft lips pressed together tightly before he smiled. "Say it."

My face was aflame.

"Please, Hollie."

And that was my undoing.

"I love you, Lucas Dayton. I have for as long as I can remember."

He exhaled what sounded like a sigh of relief. "I love you, too, Hollie Craft."

I felt my cheeks burn and realized I was smiling like a fool.

"We're here, sir," the driver called back to us.

Lucas stood and pulled out some money. "Keep the change and thank you."

"Thank you, sir! Enjoy your night!" he said in a gleeful voice.

Lucas climbed down first then reached up for me. Careful not to put weight on him, I climbed off the carriage and let him lace his fingers in mine. We climbed up the steps of his place, and I was positive all of Salem could hear the pounding of my heart in my chest.

The moment the door opened, and we both walked in, Lucas pushed me against the door and kissed me like I had never been kissed before.

It was in that moment I realized no spell could ever make a man desire a woman like Lucas Dayton desired me in that moment.

Chapter Ten

Lucas

Hollie's fingers pushed into my hair as I deepened the kiss, pushing her against my front door. I knew we should talk. Knew we should do a million other things first, but my hand moved to her thigh, lifting it until she hooked it around my body. I pressed my hard length into her, and she moaned, which caused my dick to grow harder.

My hand moved up her thigh and around to her ass. I squeezed it and pulled her body closer to mine, needing to feel her against me.

She tugged on my hair, and I nearly came undone. I wanted this woman more than I wanted my next fucking breath.

Moving my hand up the side of her body, I felt her shiver. My hand cupped her breast, and she ripped her mouth from mine. Both of us panted as I dropped my mouth and kissed her exposed cleavage.

"Oh, God, Lucas."

"Do you like that?" I asked, running my tongue along her bare skin. When I pulled it down, and her breast popped free, I groaned at the site of her nipple. My mouth covered it and sucked and teased it as she writhed against my body.

"Oh, my God," she gasped, her hands back in my hair. "More."

Smiling, I moved my hand under her skirt and slipped it into her panties. The moment I felt her wetness, I groaned and buried my face in her neck.

"You're so wet."

"Yes!" she hissed as she pulled my head back and kissed me.

My finger slid easily through her lips, and I nearly dropped to my knees when I slipped it inside. She was so fucking tight with just one finger.

"Hollie," I gasped as I broke the kiss and looked into her eyes. "I want you."

She nodded. "I want you too."

"We should... I mean... Should we talk first?"

Something moved across her face, and she started to chew nervously on her lip. "What did you want to talk about?"

"I mean, I don't know. I just don't want you to think the only thing I care about is taking you to bed. I mean, I want to take you to bed, believe me."

"Your ribs?" she asked, a look of concern on her face.

"They're fine. Are we going too fast? Should we slow down?"

She shook her head. "No, but there is something I have to tell you."

A strange feeling hit my chest, and I panicked that she was going to tell me something bad.

"Okay, what is it?"

She smiled the sweetest smile, and I could see her cheeks turn red. I had already pulled my hand out of her panties, and I moved it behind her neck, tilting her head up so she was looking me in the eyes. "Tell me, Hollie."

"I'm... I'm... I've never... I've... Well, I've never..."

Her voice trailed off, and I moved her leg off me and took a step back. Whatever she was about to tell me, she was nervous about it.

Taking her hands in mine, I kissed each one. "Tell me."

Her lips were pressed together in a tight line before she opened her mouth slightly, cleared her throat, and said, "I'm a virgin, Lucas. I've never had sex or really been past second base with anyone. You're the first man to even touch me... there."

My eyes went wide as I took another step back. "How is that possible? You're beautiful, Hollie! You've dated guys before. Surely, you've..."

It was in that moment, it hit me. I'd never seen her date anyone for very long. A few dates and that was it.

"Why?" I asked.

She shrugged. "I wanted to wait for the man I...loved."

It felt like God himself had come down from heaven and struck me with a lightning bolt. Had she been waiting for me?

Okay, wait. That was pretty fucking arrogant on my part.

"You probably think it's stupid, and I'm sure you've been with your share of women, but sex to me always felt like it was so personal. I wanted to share it with someone I knew I could give my heart to."

"And the guys you dated? None of them...?"

Her eyes looked up and met mine. "I didn't know it at the time, and to say I was saving myself and waiting for you would be a lie. But I think, deep down in my heart, I wanted them all to be you."

My heart felt like it had grown a hundred times bigger. "And you want to be with me?"

"Yes. Now. If you can, with your ribs and all."

A strangled laugh slipped free. "Trust me, I can. I'm not sure I deserve this gift, Hollie."

Tears filled her eyes. "The fact that you just called my virginity a gift... I would say you do."

Taking her hands in mine, I walked backward as I guided her through the house. "We'll go slow."

"For your ribs," she replied with a wink.

"Yes, doll, for my ribs."

Once we got into my bedroom, I walked over and turned on the side lamp. "Do you mind?"

She shook her head.

"Good, because I want to explore every inch of your body, Hollie."

Her eyes flickered with anticipation as she whispered, "Okay."

I walked up to her and ran my fingers along the bottom of her dress. Two rows of ruffles lined the bottom of it, and my dick jumped in my pants as I remembered how wet she was.

"Will you wear this again for me?"

"Do you like it?" she asked.

"I more than like it. It's sexy as fuck."

"So, what you're saying is, you're into sexy witches?"

Guiding her to the bed, I had her sit down.

"What I'm saying is, I'm into only one sexy witch, and she is currently sitting on my bed."

She smiled. "Good to know."

I slowly bent down, being sure to be careful of my ribs. I started to untie her boots, one at a time. I slipped them off and set them to the side. I ran both of my hands up her right leg until I got to the end of the stocking, then peeled it off her leg. When I went for the other one, I couldn't help but notice her breathing had increased.

"Are you nervous?" I asked as the last stocking slipped free.

Hollie shook her head while she chewed nervously on her lower lip.

"Have you ever made yourself come?" I asked as I stood back up.

She swallowed hard, and for a moment, I wasn't sure if she was going to answer me or not. She finally did.

"Yes."

"With your hand or a vibrator?"

"My hand."

I raised a brow in question. "You've never used a vibrator on yourself?"

The innocent way her face blushed made me harder than I had ever been before.

"No."

Christ. I wasn't going to last a minute when I pushed inside her.

I started to take off my costume while Hollie sat on the edge of my bed. Each article of clothing I took off, her chest rose and fell more.

"Have you ever made a man come with your hand or your mouth?"

"Second base, Lucas, only second base."

I closed my eyes. Knowing that Hollie hadn't ever been intimate with another man like that nearly made me want to fall to my knees and ask God why I deserved such a gift.

"Is there anything that is off-limits?"

She tilted her head and gave me a confused look. "Like, tying me up or something?"

I tried not to laugh, but a small chuckle slipped through. "I don't think we'll be exploring that.... At least, not right now. I was talking more like oral sex. I want to taste you, Hollie."

Her eyes closed and she moaned slightly. I was going to take that as a yes. When she opened her eyes, I smiled. "May I?"

The way her eyes locked onto my hands and watched as I reached for the button on my pants... Then when I unzipped them. And when I pulled them off, along with my boxers, Hollie sucked in a breath when my dick sprang free. It was my turn to groan when she licked her lips.

Her eyes darted up to meet mine. "I want to taste you too."

With a shake of my head, I said, "I'll come within thirty seconds if that pretty mouth of yours wraps around my cock."

Hollie's mouth dropped open into a small "O" as she stared at the appendage that bounced against my stomach. I was ready, more than ready. But I wanted her first time to be all about her needs, not mine. I had waited this long to have her; I could wait a bit longer.

"Stand up, doll."

She did as I asked. Turning her gently, I started to unzip the dress, letting it fall down her arms and straight to the floor. Hollie turned and I felt my knees go weak. She stood before me in a black lace bra and matching panties.

"You're so damn beautiful, Hollie. Your body is... It's perfect in every way."

Smiling, she reached behind her and unclasped her bra, letting it slide down her arms, then tossed it onto her dress that was now on the floor.

My hands itched to touch her. I wanted to explore every inch of her body. I reached for her breasts and cupped them both as I ran my thumb over each hardened nipple. She hissed in pleasure.

"Do you like me touching your breasts?"

Her head fell back when I pinched her nipples. "I think I just enjoy you touching me."

She was so fucking responsive to my touch. I'd only been with four women; three were one-night stands. A girl in high school whom I lost my virginity to at a graduation party, another girl I met at a bar while in college. She was three years older than me and invited me back to her place.

She knew I was inexperienced and spent most of the night teaching me how to please a woman. Then you had Wendy, whom I'd slept with maybe five times. I never felt the things I felt with any of them that I felt in that moment with Hollie.

Covering her nipple with my mouth, I gently bit on it before sucking, all the while playing with her other nipple.

"Lucas, what are you doing to me?" she gasped, her hands pushing into my hair and holding me where I was. If she liked that, she was going to really like what I was going to do next.

Letting her breast fall from my mouth, she whimpered.

"Sit down, Hollie."

Doing what I asked, she sat on the edge of my bed and went to crawl back onto it. "No, stay there."

Nodding, she started to twist her hands in that nervous motion she used. I ignored the pain in my side and got on the floor. I ran my hands up her legs and reached for her panties, giving them a slight tug so she would lift up and I could remove them. I tossed them to the side, then spread her legs open wide, moaning when I saw the light-brown patch of hair between her legs.

"Lucas," she nervously said as I pulled her to the edge of the bed.

"I promise you, it will feel good."

Her chest rose and fell.

Sliding my hand up her leg to her flat stomach, I gently pushed her back until she was lying on the bed. I placed soft kisses on the inside of each thigh until I was there. To the intimate spot that no other man had ever seen, let alone touched. Leaning down, I licked up her pussy, then sucked her clit, causing her to nearly jump off the bed.

"Holy shit!" she cried out, her hands grabbing for the bedspread.

"More?" I asked.

She lifted her head. "Please."

That word again. When she said that word, I knew I would do anything for her.

I pressed my mouth to her, licking and sucking as she bucked her hips and attempted to squirm away from me. I placed my hands on her hips and held her down. She tasted like salt and honey, and I was almost dizzy with desire for her.

"Lucas. Lucas. Oh, God, Lucas."

My name on her lips caused me to lick more, suck harder. I wanted to watch her come apart and taste what her orgasm would bring me.

Moving my hand down, I slipped one finger inside her, causing her to cry out and grab onto my hair. She pulled me closer to her and began moving her hips against my face.

"That's it, Hollie. Take it. Take it, doll."

"Lucas!" she gasped. "I'm so close."

Another finger slipped inside, and I pumped faster as I moved my mouth to her clit. I could feel her body tremble. When I lifted my eyes, our gaze caught. Mother of Christ, she was watching me.

Curling my finger, I must have hit the spot. Hollie didn't just call out my name, she screamed it, her hips bucked against my face, and she never once took her eyes off me. I could feel her contract around my fingers, and it was all I could do not to reach for my dick and pump a few times. I knew that was all it would take to come.

When her body finally stopped trembling, and her body relaxed, I withdrew my fingers and kissed the inside of her thigh.

"Did you like that?"

Her breaths were coming fast. "Like?" she gasped. "That was the most amazing thing I've ever felt. I think I left my body for a few seconds."

Smiling, I kissed her stomach and slowly got to my feet.

"Slide up the bed, Hollie. I'm going to make love to you now."

It took everything I had not to laugh when she scrambled up the bed so fast, she hit her head on the headboard.

"Ouch! Son of a bitch!"

"Are you okay?" I asked, kissing my way up her body.

"Y-yes. Your mouth feels so good on my skin."

I swirled my tongue and licked under her breasts as she bucked her hips.

"How is it possible I need more? I need more, Lucas."

Reaching for the side drawer, I pulled out a condom and rolled it on while Hollie watched.

When I looked back her, she had an expression on her face that caused me to pause.

"Do you want to stop?"

"No!" she practically cried out. "What if I'm not very good? I mean, I'm sure you've been with a lot of experienced women, and what if...?"

Her voice trailed off. Then she laughed. "I guess I could ask my sister if there is a spell to make me a good lover."

I dropped my head onto her stomach and laughed. "Hollie, I've only been with four women. Three were one-night stands, and the fourth...was a mistake."

"Wendy?" she asked, a slight edge of anger to her voice.

Not about to lie to her, I nodded.

"I hate her."

"Just don't give her another rash, okay?"

She giggled. "I don't think I did that. I mean, I didn't even say a spell."

Moving up her body, I captured her mouth with mine and kissed her thoroughly before I said, "I don't want to talk about anyone else. This is you and me right now."

She nodded and ran her fingers through my hair. "I love how soft your hair is. And your lips. They're so soft, unlike the rest of you. Your body is chiseled and solid."

I placed a kiss on her nose. "This might hurt, but I'm going to be as gentle as I can."

Drawing in a deep breath, she nodded.

Slipping my hand between her legs, I slipped two fingers in. She was soaking wet. I moved them while I worked her clit with my thumb.

"That feels so good," she moaned as she lifted her hips. "I want to feel you, Lucas. I need to feel you."

Removing my fingers, I positioned my dick at her entrance and barely pushed inside of her while I still worked her clit. My mouth found hers as she wrapped her arms around me.

Rubbing my dick against her entrance, I worked her clit until she ripped her mouth from me. "I'm going to come again."

When she shattered, I pushed inside her some. She tensed, but I worked her clit again, and I was pretty sure another orgasm hit because I could feel her pussy trying to pull me in. I pushed in more.

"Jesus," she called out as she dug her nails into my shoulders. "More. Lucas! More."

With one last push, I broke through the barrier, and Hollie froze.

"Are you okay?" I asked with a strangled voice. She felt so fucking good, I couldn't move. Her pussy was contracting still, and if I moved, I was positive I'd come, and it would be over before it started.

"I'm okay. You can move," she said as she wrapped her legs around me.

When I didn't move, she looked at me. "Lucas?"

"Give me a second. If I move, it might be over."

She dug her teeth into her lower lip to try and hide her smile.

Placing her hand on the side of my face, she reached up and kissed me. I pulled out some and slowly pushed back in. I did it a few more times until we both found a rhythm, working together in a way I had never experienced before. It was as if her body knew what it needed, what it wanted, and she followed it.

"Oh, Lucas. It feels so good," she whispered against my ear as I dropped my head and tried not to come.

"Hollie, baby, I need to go faster."

"Yes. Faster. Can you go harder?"

I stopped moving and met her eyes. I was never letting this woman go. Never.

Chapter Eleven

Hollie

Lucas paused and looked down at me, his eyes dark with lust and desire. "Tell me if it hurts."

I wrapped my legs around him tighter, pulling him all the way into me. "It won't. I just feel like I need more."

He looked as if he might not move again. Then he moved, and I was taken to heaven once again. He reached for my leg, pulling it up and causing my body to move so that he could go deeper. It felt glorious.

"Yes! Oh, God, yes!"

Then he went faster. My hips moved to meet his, our bodies slapping together and making the most erotic sound I'd ever heard, not that I'd heard many. I watched a few porn movies in my time, but nothing could have prepared me for this.

"Hollie," he said as he seemed to lose control. Yes, yes, yes. I loved it. I loved that he was losing himself inside me.

"Lucas, I'm so close. I'm so..."

And then it happened. He hit something deep inside me, and I exploded. I never thought I would be the type of woman to cry out a man's name when I came, but holy hell and the saints above. I came so hard, I saw stars burst in the room.

His name tumbled from my mouth, and then I swore I felt him grow bigger inside me.

"I'm going to come, Hollie. Fuck, I'm going to come."

"Yes!" I cried out as I pulled his mouth to mine. He moaned as pumped into me faster, his body going tight and almost rigid. Then he started to slow down until he stopped. His breathing sounded like he had just run a race as he held his body ever so slightly off mine. I wanted to pull him down onto me. I needed to feel the weight of him, but I was also struggling to breath in air.

When we both were finally able to speak, our eyes met.

"When can we do that again?" I asked.

Lucas laughed and gently pulled out of me. I winced at the slight pain, but it went away as quickly as it had come.

"I don't want to make you sore."

"Trust me, if you make me come like that even once more, I won't care how sore I am."

He rolled off me and lay on his back, drawing in a few deep breaths. "As much as I'd love to say I'll be ready to go here in a minute, it might take a bit."

Moving to his side, he rested his head on his hand. "How about a hot bath? I don't know if they really work after you've lost your virginity, but I've read it before."

"Me too," I said as I moved and sat on him. He was still hard and still had the condom on. "Next time, I'm on top."

He closed his eyes and let out a whimper, and I felt his dick stir under me. I moved and it stirred again. "Are you sure you're not ready for round two?"

Laughing, he sat up and hugged me as he pressed his mouth to mine. The kiss was soft and sweet. Slower than it had been minutes ago and filled with so much more than just the desire to make both of us feel good.

When he pulled back, I rested my forehead against his and ran my fingers through his hair. "I always dreamed my first time would be amazing, but I never thought it would be anything like this. I've never experienced an orgasm like the ones you gave me tonight with my hand."

He grinned and seemed to look proud. "I've got a few other ways I'd like to outdo myself."

"Is that so?" I asked with a raised brow. "Tell me?"

"I'll tell you all the ways I've dreamed of making love to you."

I nodded.

"Slowly, like we just did. In the shower. Up against a wall. From behind. You on top. In public."

"In public?" I asked as I slapped his chest.

"Yes. In my car, on my office desk, in my office chair."

Laughing, I said, "You've really dreamed of taking me like that? All those ways and all those places?"

"I don't know how to tell you this, Hollie, but the first time I ever jerked myself off, it was to a picture of you when I was thirteen in my bedroom."

My mouth dropped open before I started to laugh.

"Come on," he softly said. "Let's go take a shower, and then I want to hold you while we fall asleep."

I stretched and felt every muscle in my body as well as the slight pain between my legs. After waking Lucas up around three in the morning, we made love, then talked for nearly two hours until we both fell asleep, utterly exhausted.

The smell of coffee and bacon had me sitting up. A moment of panic hit as I realized I had three events today I needed to be overseeing. Reaching for my cell, I sighed when I saw it was only six-thirty.

Slipping out of Lucas's bed, I made my way over to his dresser and opened the drawer I had seen him get a T-shirt out of last night. I pulled out one and slipped it over my head. It fell to the tops of my thighs. About to search for my panties, I smiled and decided to go sans underwear and made my way down to his kitchen.

As I drew closer, I heard Lucas speaking to someone.

"Manny, we need to get as much out and documented as we can before the first snow hits. Plus, the city is already behind on the construction of the park. I know it's the crack-ass of dawn, and I know you have a hangover. I'm aware of that, but it is not my fault the ball was on a Sunday night and not a Saturday."

I watched Lucas as he flipped pancakes in the air, then tended to the bacon. Oh, yes, the man was sexy as hell in the kitchen. The sweatpants that hung low on his hips helped with the overall sex appeal. What topped it all was the bare feet. I pressed my lips tightly together to keep from moaning. Was it bad that I wanted him again? To be honest, I could go back to his bed and stay there for the next week if I thought we could.

Walking up to him, he turned and flashed me a smile that would have made my panties melt, had I been wearing any. I reached for the bowl of eggs he was about to beat for what I was guessing were scrambled eggs.

"I'll be there in about an hour or so, and to sweeten the deal, I'll bring coffee."

Lucas smiled and leaned down to give me a kiss before ending his call.

"See you soon."

"You have a busy day, I see," I said as I beat the eggs and then sprayed the pan Lucas had set aside for the eggs.

"We're only working half a day so that some of the people who have kids can leave early for Halloween tonight."

After I poured the eggs into the pan, I walked over to the sink. "That's sweet of you."

"Don't give me too much credit. I want to be there for Greg's proposal tonight."

Laughing, I rinsed the bowl and placed it in the dishwasher.

"You've got a pretty busy day with... How many events?"

"Three, but one of them, we set up on Friday, and I don't need to be there for it. The other one is a birthday party, and my assistant Lynn is handling most of that since I wanted to really focus on Greg's. I just need to swing by and make sure everything is right."

He tilted his head and watched me as I poured a cup of coffee. "You really love your job, don't you?"

Nodding, I replied, "I do. I've always loved planning parties."

"I don't know if I've ever told you this before, but you're damn good at it. I've been to a few city functions you helped organize, and every time, people have bragged about how good you are at your job. The city Christmas luncheon last year for the employees who were retiring was stunning."

"You were there?" I asked before I took a sip of the hot coffee.

"I was. My former director retired last year. I saw you a few times at the beginning, walking around with a clipboard and a little headset."

My face heated. "I don't often stay at the events unless I'm asked to. At bigger events like that, they want to make sure someone is there in case something goes bad."

Lucas turned and flipped another pancake, then started to take the bacon out of the frying pan. I made my way over to the scrambled eggs and tended to them.

"What are your favorite events?"

I exhaled. "Oh, man, that's a hard one. I think engagements are right up there with holiday parties."

"Which holiday?"

"Any!" I said with a giggle. "There is something about the holidays that I just love."

"Favorite holiday?" he asked, setting a plate full of pancakes on the island bar, followed by the bacon. I scooped the eggs out of the pan into a bowl Lucas had handed me.

"Halloween has always been one of my favorites."

"It's that witch inside of you," he said with a wink.

"Maybe! Christmas is my second favorite. Then I would have to say, St. Patrick's Day."

Lucas laughed. "Why?"

We both sat down and started to make our plates. "Hello! No one can throw a party like the Irish. I can't tell you how many times I've done a St. Patrick's Day event and have nearly gotten trashed during it. They're always so fun."

He nodded. "I've been to some pretty fun parties. Okay, which one next? Valentine's Day?"

Screwing up my face, I shook my head. "I can't stand that holiday."

Lucas's eyes went wide. "Why not?"

I gave a half-shoulder shrug and prayed he didn't see the lie on my face. My prayer, unfortunately, went unanswered.

"You're lying. Tell me why you don't like it."

"It's nothing, Lucas."

He reached for my hand. "Please."

I looked down at my plate of food and moved the eggs around with my fork. Not looking up at him, I spoke. "Our freshman year of high school, they had a sign-up to send a rose to your special valentine."

"I remember that. It stopped after that year, though, and I never found out why."

My eyes jerked up to look at him. "You didn't know?"

"Know what?"

"A bunch of girls decided it would be fun to send me and Sarah black roses with some pretty cruel things written on them. Someone went so far as to put a dead mouse on one and put it in my locker."

Lucas looked horrified. "I heard about that! I didn't know it had happened to you and Sarah, though."

"A couple of other girls as well. They all practiced witchcraft or have parents who did. Even though I didn't, it was association through my sister."

"Did they ever find out who put the dead mouse in your locker?"

My eyes met his, and I really didn't want to tell him.

"It doesn't matter. It was so long ago."

"Hollie, who did it?"

I chewed nervously on my lower lip before I looked away and said, "Wendy."

"Wendy? Wendy Hoffman?"

With a tight smile, I replied, "The one and only."

"No wonder you can't stand her. I never knew she did that to you."

"She did a lot of things to me, Lucas. But by the end of our sophomore year, I learned to stand up to her. Plus, I might have told her I was going to put a hex on her. She pretty much left me alone after that. Although, I'm pretty sure Sarah did put a hex on her, even though she will deny it until she takes her last breath."

"I'm so sorry, Hollie. I had no idea she treated you poorly."

"It's okay. It's all water under the bridge."

He reached for my hand and squeezed it. "I hate that we wasted so much time being so stupid."

Smiling, I replied, "I think it worked out the way it was supposed to."

Our eyes locked and I wondered if Lucas could feel the way the air sparkled between us.

I stood. "Let's clean up. We both have a busy day ahead of us."

"You get the dishes, and I'll get the pans. I'm a messy cook and tend to use more things than I need to."

Chuckling, I took our dishes and headed to the kitchen sink. I rinsed and placed items in the dishwasher as Lucas cleaned up the kitchen. When he made his way back over to me, he wrapped his arms around me.

"I haven't mentioned how incredibly sexy you are in my T-shirt."

My head dropped back to his chest. "I hope you don't mind."

"Not at all."

When his hand touched my thigh, I felt my breath catch in my throat and my heartbeat pick up. He slowly moved his hand up, and when he realized I wasn't wearing any panties, he dropped his head to mine and let out a low-sounding growl.

"If I had known you weren't wearing panties, we would have never made it through breakfast."

I turned in his arms and wrapped them around his neck. "What would you have eaten then if you had let all that food go to waste?"

His eyes darkened. "You."

My tongue instantly ran over my lips as my gaze dropped to his mouth. I could feel the rush of wetness between my legs.

"Too bad there isn't dessert after breakfast."

Lucas narrowed his eyes and replied in a husky voice, "That's not a rule, you know."

"It's not?" I asked innocently.

He lifted me up and placed me on the kitchen island, pushing my legs apart. "Hold onto the sides and don't touch me, Hollie."

"What?" I asked, my voice sounding as if I just ran a marathon.

"Hold onto the edges of the island and do not touch me."

Swallowing hard, I did as he said. He bent down and I knew he was trying to keep his pain off his face. I was about to say something when he pushed a finger in, and I gasped and nearly jumped off the island.

"Fuck, you're wet."

All I could do was nod. Then he was there. His mouth on me, licking and sucking like he was about to eat his last meal. My head dropped back, and I gripped the edges of the kitchen island so hard, my hands nearly cramped.

"Lucas, yes! Don't stop, I'm so close."

He buried his face deeper, and I let out a strangled cry of pleasure.

My hand went to his hair, and I pulled him in closer. Then he stopped and I looked down at him.

"Why did you stop?" I panted.

"You touched me."

Frowning, I lifted my hand and cursed it. Holding onto the island again, Lucas went straight to my clit. When his fingers filled me, I knew my orgasm was coming. I could feel it in the tips of my toes.

"More!" I cried as I rocked my hips against my face. Who was I and how did Lucas bring out this side of me?

"Yes! Yes! Oh, God! Lucas!" I cried out as my orgasm hit me like a bolt of lightning.

I wasn't even sure what I was saying. All I knew was it felt so damn good, and I never wanted to leave this spot ever again.

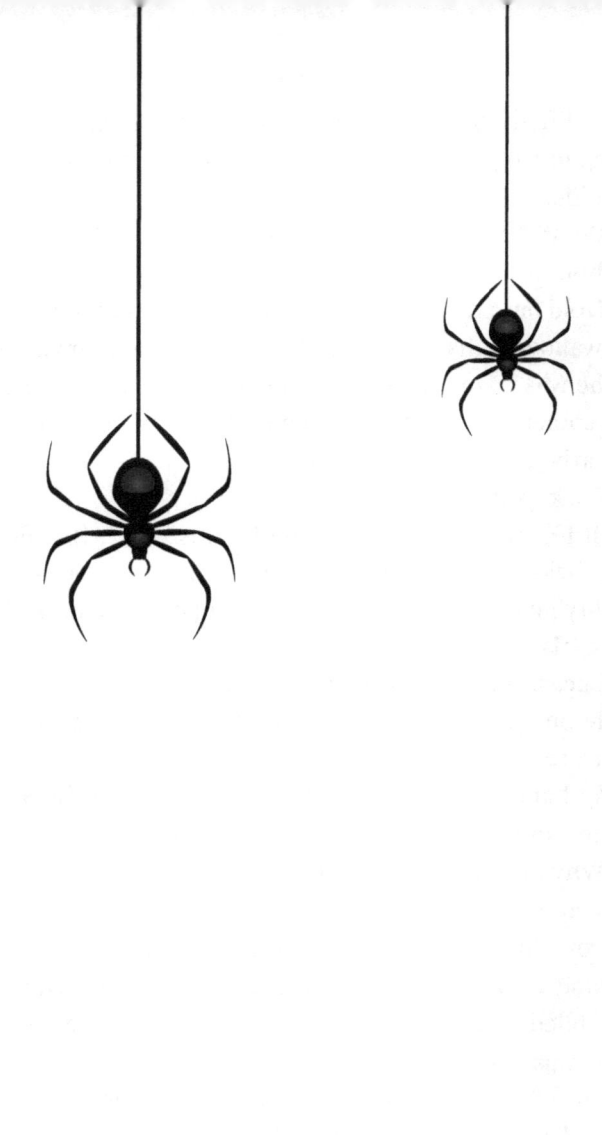

Chapter Twelve

Lucas

What a day.

After a successful day at the dig site, I left to help with the last of the setup for Greg and Janet's engagement. I loved seeing Hollie in action and had caught myself a number of times daydreaming about last night and this morning. After everything had been set up, I snuck into the barn office and kissed Hollie until she was left dizzy and wanting more. She hadn't planned on staying for the celebration afterward, but I had insisted. I wanted everyone to know that we were together now and that Hollie Craft was officially off the market and mine. She wouldn't let me pick her up at her place because she said she still had a ton of stuff to do and would be late for the party, so we made plans to meet up.

"It was so beautiful!" my mother gushed as she hugged me. "Greg and Janet can't stop smiling, and it's all because of you and Hollie."

"You should save the hugs for Hollie. She was the one who turned this entire barn into this," I said as I swung my arm out to the decorated barn.

"She is amazing, isn't she?" Mom asked.

I couldn't stop the smile even if I had tried. "She really is."

"I couldn't help but notice how the two of you seemed to be closer than normal today. I think, at one point, you might have even snuck off with her."

My smile grew into a full-on grin. "Let's just say, we called a truce, and things are really good between us."

Mom could hardly contain her excitement as she let out a little yelp, then clapped. She reached up and kissed me on the cheek.

"I always knew you two would end up together. I saw you both at the ball last night."

I rubbed the back of my neck as I looked around, then focused back on my mother. "Mom, don't get crazy with this, okay?"

Her face fell. "Is it not serious?"

"Oh, it is. I mean, I really like Hollie. A lot. So please don't be pushy, okay?"

She gasped and clutched her hand to her chest. "Me? Pushy? I wouldn't dream of doing that."

I raised a single brow. "If you say so."

"Oh, I see your Uncle Nate. I'll be right back, darling."

Once my mother walked away, I pulled out my phone and sent Hollie a text.

Me: ETA of when you'll be here?

A loud bang came from across the room, and I looked up. Someone had fallen into one of the food tables.

"Shit," I said as I rushed over to help.

"I'm so sorry! I lost my balance while trying to show Dan here how long I could stand on one leg," my Aunt Nancy stated as my father was helping her up.

"Thank you, Tim, darling. You're such a good brother and thank goodness you're a doctor. I think I broke something."

"Your ego, dear sister," my father said with a smile as he shook his head at his sister.

"What happened?" I asked as I bent down to pick up some plates and food that had spilled over.

My father rolled his eyes. "Your aunt was just showing us proof that she was once a flamingo in a previous life by standing on one foot. Unfortunately, she lost her balance after five seconds."

"It was at least ten!" Aunt Nancy called out as I attempted to hide my smile.

"You okay, Aunt Nancy?" I asked as I picked up the last of the bad food and tossed it into the garbage that was being held open.

With a wave of her hand and then a thumbs-up, she made her way over to the punch, which I was positive my father spiked.

A light tap on my shoulder had me turning around, a smile on my face.

When I saw it was Wendy, my smile faded. "Wendy," I said as I looked at her hand that was extended out.

With a smile that said she was up to no good, she purred, "You dropped your phone, honey."

I took it and cleared my throat. "I'm not your honey, Wendy."

She leaned in and ran her tongue over her top teeth. "You are when you let me suck that big cock of yours."

I cringed at the image and her words. "Is there something you wanted?"

She laughed. "Besides you?"

"I see the rash is clearing up."

Her smile faded and she reached up to touch her face. "I think that little witch had something to do with it."

"Little witch?" I asked.

"Hollie! She must have told her sister to sell me some bad products. It's not a coincidence my body broke out after I used a soap her sister recommended I try."

"Really? It could be, especially if you've never used it before."

Her mouth opened to argue, but it was clear she hadn't been prepared for me to be alone.

"Lucas, do you have a moment where we could talk? It's not personal, more on the side of business."

I laughed. "Business? What could we possibly have in common when it came to that?"

A look of hurt moved over her face before it disappeared.

She looked around. "Can we go somewhere quiet?"

A strange feeling swept over me, and I knew if I went anywhere with Wendy Hoffman, I would be in a heap of trouble.

"Whatever you need to say, you can say it here."

She sighed. "Fine. Rumor has it you're involved with Hollie Craft. I stopped by earlier to see if I could help set up and saw the two of you coming out of the office together, and it was clear to everyone looking that something was going on between the two of you."

"And that's a problem why?"

"She's crazy, Locus. Did you know she's now claiming to be a witch? Just like her nutty sister and aunt."

I didn't say anything. Instead, I slipped my hands into my pant pockets.

"Lucas, you hold a very prominent position with the city. What if they found out you were dating someone who thought she was a...a witch?"

Leaning in closer, I asked, "You do know what town we live in, Wendy, right? The mayor practices witchcraft. Besides, doesn't your mom dabble with crystals?"

"She most certainly does not!"

I let out a frustrated sigh. "Listen, Wendy, whatever you have to say about Hollie isn't going to work. We're dating. I don't care if she thinks she is a poodle. So, if you're done, I'm going to excuse myself. My girlfriend just walked in."

Whipping her head toward the front door, Wendy gasped, then turned back to me. "You're dating her? You're honestly dating her?" Wendy let out a disbelieving laugh. "You hate her!"

I took a step closer to Wendy. "You have her mistaken for you. I don't care that your sister is now engaged to my brother. If you so much as look at Hollie the wrong way, you will regret it."

Her mouth fell open, and she stared at me with a shocked expression before it turned cold. "Is that a threat?"

I stood up tall, took a couple of steps back, and then winked. "That is a promise."

The feel of soft, warm lips on my body caused me to roll over and smile the moment I saw Hollie kneeling on my bed with a cup of coffee in her hand.

"Good morning, sleeping beauty," she purred before leaning down and giving me a quick kiss on the lips before moving back so I could sit up.

I scrubbed my hand down my face and yawned. "What time is it?"

"It's six-thirty. I think you forgot to set your alarm."

Taking the coffee, I took a drink and sighed. "Thank God you're up at the crack of dawn every day. I've got a meeting this morning."

Giving me a wink, Hollie said, "You're welcome. I've already gone for a short run on your treadmill and showered.

Want me to make you a smoothie while you hop in the shower?"

"That would be amazing. I'll take this with me."

She giggled and headed out of my bedroom.

After showering and putting a suit on, since the meeting was with city officials, I made my way to the kitchen. I had heard the blender going a little bit ago, but now, the house was silent. Hollie wasn't in the kitchen, and when I called out, she didn't answer.

The smoothie was in the freezer, and when I glanced out the back window, I saw Hollie standing out there, staring into the backyard.

"Hey," I said as I stepped out onto my back patio. "It's freezing out here."

Hollie turned and had tears in her eyes. My entire world nearly dropped out from under me. I rushed over to her. "What's wrong?"

She slowly shook her head, opened her mouth to speak, then shut it.

"Hollie, baby, talk to me."

When her eyes lifted to mine, I saw something I never wanted to see there. Pain.

"What's wrong?"

Without saying a word, Hollie handed me her phone. A part of me told me not to take it. To not even look at what it was she wanted me to see.

"Wendy sent me a little gift."

When I hit play on the video, my knees nearly buckled out from under me. Looking back at Hollie, I wanted to throw the phone when I saw the tears streaming down her face.

The only thing I could say came out in a voice that didn't even sound like my own. It was filled with regret and shame.

"Hollie," I whispered as she pushed past me and fled.

To be continued in

coming December 25, 2022.

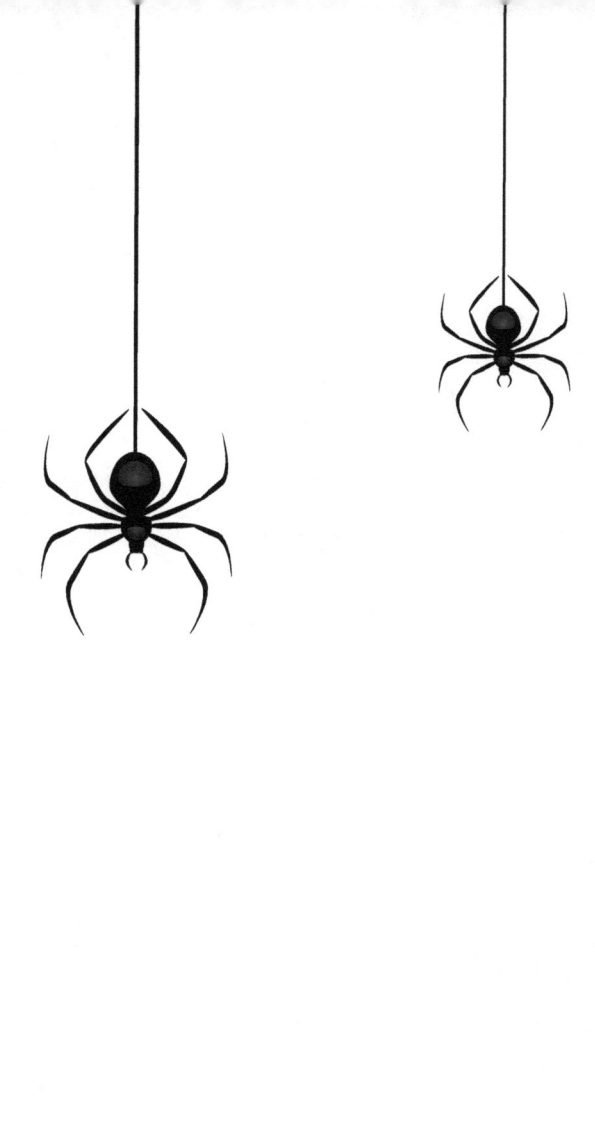

Other Books by Kelly Elliott

Holidaze in Salem
A Bit of Hocus Pocus
A Bit of Holly Jolly – December 25, 2022
A Bit of Wee Luck – March 17, 2023
A Bit of Razzle Dazzle – July 4, 2023

Love in Montana
Fearless Enough – March 21, 2023
Cherished Enough – June 6, 2023
Brave Enough – August 29, 2023
Daring Enough – November 21, 2023
Loved Enough – February 6, 2024
Forever Enough – April 30, 2024
Enchanted Enough – July 23, 2024
Perfect Enough – October 15, 2024
Devoted Enough – January 7, 2025

The Seaside Chronicles
Returning Home*
Part of Me*
Lost to You
Someone to Love - January 3, 2023
*Available on audiobook at time of print

Stand Alones

The Journey Home
Who We Were*
The Playbook*
Made for You*
*Available on audiobook

Boggy Creek Valley Series

The Butterfly Effect*
Playing with Words*
She's the One*
Surrender to Me*
Hearts in Motion (releases on March 22, 2022)
Looking for You (releases on May 3, 2022)
Surprise Novella TBD
*Available on audiobook

Meet Me in Montana Series

Never Enough*
Always Enough*
Good Enough*
Strong Enough*
*Available on audiobook

Southern Bride Series

Love at First Sight*
Delicate Promises*
Divided Interests*
Lucky in Love*
Feels Like Home *
Take Me Away*
Fool for You*
Fated Hearts*
*Available on audiobook

Cowboys and Angels Series

Lost Love
Love Profound
Tempting Love
Love Again
Blind Love
This Love
Reckless Love
*Series available on audiobook

Boston Love Series

Searching for Harmony
Fighting for Love
*Series available on audiobook

Austin Singles Series

Seduce Me
Entice Me
Adore Me
*Series available on audiobook

Wanted Series

Wanted*
Saved*
Faithful*
Believe
Cherished*
A Forever Love*
The Wanted Short Stories
All They Wanted
*Available on audiobook

Love Wanted in Texas Series
Spin-off series to the WANTED Series
Without You
Saving You
Holding You
Finding You
Chasing You
Loving You
Entire series available on audiobook
*Please note *Loving You* combines the last book
of the Broken and Love Wanted in Texas series.

Broken Series
*Broken**
*Broken Dreams**
*Broken Promises**
Broken Love
*Available on audiobook

The Journey of Love Series
Unconditional Love
Undeniable Love
Unforgettable Love
*Entire series available on audiobook

With Me Series
Stay With Me
Only With Me
*Series available on audiobook

Speed Series

Ignite

Adrenaline

*Series available on audiobook or coming to audiobook
soon*

COLLABORATIONS

Predestined Hearts (co-written with Kristin Mayer)*

Play Me (co-written with Kristin Mayer)*

*Dangerous Temptations (*co-written with Kristin Mayer*

*Available on audiobook